Remi is the first human-Rrassic hybrid, and she leaves the creche to return to Imrahl with her nearest four siblings. All of them have been trained to fight, spy, and make themselves useful to the war effort.

Hiding her existence from the unmated humans hadn't occurred to her, and she is soon without a proper place and in a holding pattern. A job as a bodyguard is a great distraction.

Kromir is the Mrek-Rrassic who has been sent to examine the exotic new human-Saya. His bodyguard is one of the new species and therefore out of his grasp until he finds out that she isn't, and she isn't.

She leads him to the creche, and he sees the army that is rising around them, her brothers and sisters, and as she calls them, her cousins. He needs to report back to the council, but he needs proof. Remi is an excellent specimen, so he takes her along . . . for science.

This book is a work of fiction. Names, characters, places, and incidents either are products of the author's imagination or are used fictitiously. Any resemblance to actual events or locales or persons, living or dead, is entirely coincidental.

Inheriting War
Copyright © 2019 Viola Grace
ISBN: 978-1-4874-2476-3
Cover art by Angela Waters

Published by eXtasy Books Inc or
Devine Destinies, an imprint of eXtasy Books Inc
Look for us online at:
www.eXtasybooks.com or www.devinedestinies.com

Inheriting War
Brace for Humanity Book 6

By

Viola Grace

OTHER BOOKS IN THIS SERIES

CHAPTER ONE

Remi struck out and used the stun sticks she was wielding to disable her opponent. The huge gelatin-like Voboth simulation buckled and dissolved before disappearing.

Remi deactivated and stowed her sticks in the sheaths strapped to her thighs. When that was done, she leaned over with her hands on her knees and breathed heavily.

"Well done, Remi. You have trained beyond my wildest dreams."

She straightened and turned to face her father. "Thank you, Dad. It means a lot."

Remi left the mat with her brothers and sisters fighting hard in the background. Her parents had managed their twenty children, and each and every one of them was surging toward adulthood twice as fast as the other canister-born.

Arix gave her a hug, and he walked with her out of the training centre. "Your mother has a big meal planned."

Remi smiled. "Of course, she does. Five of her little ones are leaving tomorrow."

"We have been waiting for this day and yet hoped it wouldn't come."

"It is the sole reason for my existence, and I am very grateful that it was you two who were my parents."

"And we are grateful that you were the first to arrive. If Tomos had been the first, I think we might have stopped at one."

Remi chuckled and elbowed her father lightly. Her broth-

1

er Tomos was younger than she was by four months, and then, the triplets had arrived. Tomos was at the edge of his Nool phase into a Luthin, and Ari, Arrow, and Arel were about a year away from their transformations into Zjin, Regiz, and Luthin.

Communication with the Rrassic council had determined that the boys should get back to Imrahl before they finished their transformations. It would be easier to see the details of their changes as no human-Rrassic had ever been a Nool before.

The boys could pass for actual Rrassic, but Remi was in a bit of a conundrum. She was taller than her mother by a head, had been in combat training since she could walk, and was an excellent hunter and tracker. Her status as the first hybrid was the only thing that made her desirable.

"Would it be horrible to say that I wished I could stay?"

Her father chuckled. "No. I also wish you to remain, but it isn't ideal. You can help so many people, Remi, simply by being yourself."

She wrinkled her nose. "I know. I just wonder about the place for the female hybrids. There is no place in Rrassic society for women who can fight like we can."

"You will make a place. I know you, Remi. You have the heart of a fighter and the soul of a dancer. You will find a path that your sisters and cousins can tread, and you will burn it into our society."

She laughed. "Is that all?"

"And then, you will bake cookies." He winked at her, and she giggled. They nudged themselves back and forth on the walkway to the building on the beach that the hybrids called home.

"I do like making cookies."

"I am aware of it. If I didn't have lessons with the littles every day, I would weigh ten pounds more."

She looked at her father, his gold-green skin and his kind eyes. "You don't look a day older than you did when I was decanted."

He smiled. "You remember?"

"I do. I was named while Aunt Niiva was holding me, and later, Aunt Sarah held me and told me that I would do great things."

"Did she say anything else?"

"She said I was clever." The imprint from her thoughts had been bright.

"We wrote to her a few years ago, and she has returned a note that she has a place for you."

"Does she know I am grown?"

He nodded. "They know that you are coming back as adults. In Imrahl time, we will join you in a week or ten days."

"I know I have been trained to calculate time, but it is still peculiar."

"As long as you know you will never arrive before you left, all will be fine." He chuckled. "It will be years before we see you again, but I want you to be well, be happy, and be strong."

"I will try." She wanted to say more, but her mother came out and gave her a huge hug, urging her into the house that overlooked the beach and the enormous ocean where she had swum for the first time.

All the memories that she had would have to comfort her when she was on her own. One day on Imrahl was four years in the creche. The luck of the Rrassic researchers to find just such a dimensional pocket was her curse.

"Did you enjoy your combat practice?" Bree smiled and led her into the kitchen.

"I did, but then, I always do. Are you going to be all right without me here?"

"I knew from the moment that I met your father that our children would be something special, and I also knew that I wasn't going to have a human life with you. So, now, we are all more than we were destined to be, and we are going to have new lives when we get back to Imrahl in fifteen years when all of our little ones are grown."

Remi smiled when her father entered the kitchen and got to work. They moved together, shifting, chopping, and flipping the ingredients around in a dance they had done since she was five while her body developed at twice the normal rate.

Her mother's gift had been to impart rapid development to all of her children. The other children in the creche were developing normally. The three children from the Lianne-Sorrok line were her nearest cousins, and they would be leaving one Imrahl day after she and her brothers did.

The youngest cousin had arrived eight years earlier, and the sober little girl was just as charming today as she had been the day she was decanted. Alia Sarah-Lekorh was currently at her history lesson. Alia was the only one who never asked about her parents, she said it was because she could still feel them.

Smiling and humming, Remi realized that if anyone could keep in touch with their child, it would be Sarah and her mate.

In her lessons, Remi had learned that the Saya should not even have been able to have children. The altered human clones had characteristics that none of the Rrassic had anticipated.

It was rather fun to be a hybrid of a species that they were breeding as cannon fodder to protect the pure Rrassic. They had no idea what they had created.

Remi went to set the table, but her brothers were already in and moving around with practiced ease. Everybody did the same chores, and it was only when you exhibited a talent for cooking that you got to spend time in the kitchen with mum.

Today was the last day she would see them until her mom and dad went back to Imrahl and more caretakers and canisters were brought to the creche.

The older children were all in their Nool state, and everyone was waiting for the day where they could leave to meet their parents. Part of Remi's job was to arrange dwellings for all of the hybrids as they left their world for the more fixed planet of Imrahl. They had been bred for war, and they were ready for it. It was one hell of an inheritance.

Remi stood on the launch with her brothers and kept her eyes forward, to the portal. Her family encompassed nearly all types of birth that were possible for the hybrids. There was an individual female, individual male, and multiples. The only type that they didn't have were identical twins, but there were only three examples of that, and they were all in primary development and physically less than twelve years old. They had been a later shipment to the creche.

She watched the platform rise to the portal and kept her head high. They would spend three heartbeats in between to step down the speed of their lives into that of Imrahl. Those three heartbeats were going to feel like forever.

Remi looked at her brothers, and they were all pretending to be impassive, but tiny ticks around their bodies gave them away. One had a corner of his mouth curling upward, another made a fist, Tomos' eyes were narrowed, and Arrow's body was nearly humming in place from tension.

She inhaled deeply as they entered the portal, and she stepped forward, finding the platform inside the edge. When she started to walk, she counted her heartbeats. One. Everything was dark around her; it felt like the world was spinning wildly and she had no way to feel what or who was next to her. Two. Slashes of light made their way through the maelstrom and began to dance along her skin. Three. The whine of sound twisted and went from a high pitch into a low hum as she continued to walk. Four. She stepped out of the portal and walked onto the receiving deck, keeping moving because her brothers were going to walk out after her.

She listened for the footfalls, the light ahead of her keeping her eyes from focusing. She counted as all of her brothers stepped forward, and when they were through, she walked up to the Dorbin-Rrassic that was standing and staring.

"Overseer Iktabi, we are the first children of Bree-Arix, hybrids of human-Rrassic at your service."

The overseer's companion covered her mouth and tears came to her eyes. "I just saw you last week, Remi."

Remi grinned. "I am aware of it, Isabella. You wore silver and blue to my decanting."

She was a head taller than the human woman, and Isabella was staring. "You can look at my features all you like once medical has worked my brothers and me over."

Overseer Iktabi smiled, and he extended his hand. "Remi, welcome home."

Remi clasped his forearm as she had been trained to by her live instructors and the simulations. His eyes widened, and a slow smile spread. "You are all trained?"

"We are all trained."

She made the introductions, and Isabella was surprised. "All of you are adults. It has only been a week."

Tomos raised his brows and smiled. "If you say so, Aunt."

Isabella blinked. "Aunt?"

Remi filled in. "Mother said that we should give honorifics to the mated women who have had children growing in the creche. Aunt and Uncle were the terms that were eventually decided on."

"How will you decide on who qualifies?"

Remi smiled slowly. "We will know. None of the un-mated ladies will hear it from us. The honorific will only be used with those who know who we are and what we are. I know that I do not appear to be a standard-issue human, so we will have to play it by ear when it comes to me."

Isabella smiled. "You sound like your mother."

"Good. I have had to listen to her for quite a while." Remi chuckled. "So, shall we get to medical for a full scan of what we have become?"

Iktabi was speaking to her brothers with a slight smile on his face. He nodded slightly, and Isabella beamed. "Right. Off we go."

Remi nodded to her brothers, and they straightened, following her out of the port behind the overseer and his mate, and out into the streets of the one city of Imrahl.

They had heard about this place since they could speak, and now, they were finally here. Ready to serve the Rrassic empire.

CHAPTER TWO

Disarming herself was to be understood, but the gathered crowd of everyone with any kind of medical degree was a little off-putting. Remi stepped into the scanner, and it was calibrated for her height and weight. Her brothers stood by with their hands behind their backs, feet slightly apart. They were ready if anyone got grabby.

The scanners ran up and down, light invaded her to the cellular level, and finally, the machine let her free.

She stepped free, and one of the medics prepared an injection. She paused when he gave her the stabilization jab that she needed after moving through the portal.

She stood aside with her other siblings while Tomos went in for his scans. He was on the cusp of finishing his transformation to Luthin, and their father was very proud of him.

Her aunt Sarah glided up next to her, wearing the hood of the Saya. "It is good to see you again, Remi."

"It is nice to be back. I can hardly wait until Mother and Father return with the others."

"It will be soon by our measurement of time. Lianne and Sorrok are preparing to go with Niiva and Argo. Niiva might not be up for parentage, but she is an excellent physical trainer."

"Argo is very attentive. He will be a good role model for the children."

Remi felt the whisper in her thoughts. A curl of energies that were not her own was seeking information. Remi opened her mind to Sarah and let her look.

"Oh. I am sorry." Sarah blushed.

"I felt you in my mind on my birthday as well. It felt the same then."

"You did?"

"I did. My brothers would have, too. We share a way of thinking."

"I cannot believe how many children your parents have had."

Remi smiled. "Alia is growing up very well. She will be here in ten days."

Sarah smiled. "Is she really?"

"Yes. Her third eye hasn't opened yet, but we are confident that it will."

Remi brought up her memory of Alia Sarah-Lekorh, and she showed her to her mother. Alia was doing math and laughing, the third eye still firmly closed.

Sarah swayed, and Remi caught her.

The human-Saya smiled weakly. "She looks like her father."

Lekorh came toward them and took possession of his mate. "She does look like me. I don't know whether to be pleased or appalled. Her communications are never that specific about her appearance."

Remi blinked. "You communicate with her?"

Sarah smiled slightly. "In flashes. She likes help with math. Lekorh gets the problems in a burst, and he sends back most of the answer but leaves out a vital bit."

Remi was amazed. "How does that work?"

Lekorh chuckled. "Speed of thought. I don't know if I am helping her in the moment or if she is getting the answers months later, but we both enjoy the contact."

Remi smiled. "She never said a thing."

Sarah grinned. "He wasn't sure what was going on at first. He thought I was asking him if I could stay up later."

They were having an interesting moment while Remi's brothers continued to cycle through their checks and injections.

When Arrow was done with his checks, she turned and looked back to the medics. "So, are we cleared to enter the city?"

Iktabi nodded. "Your brothers will be taken to the Nool quarters and oriented for their new positions."

Remi noted a lack of inclusion. "What about me?"

"You are going to be installed at the VIP building until the representative from the Rrassic council arrives."

The murmur that went through the med centre was unmistakable.

Remi nodded. "Of course. Just a moment." She went and hugged each of her brothers, and then, she reset her weapons.

Being separated from her siblings was part of the deal. She had been born to prove the effectiveness of the human genome mixing with that of the Rrassic, so she was the ambassador for her family's genetics.

She looked at Tomos, and he nodded then gave her a wink. "Take care of yourself, Remi. We are going to be scoping out the humans who have yet to make a decision."

She put her hand over her face and groaned. "This is going to come back to bite our mother in the ass."

He grinned. "Father will protect her."

She muttered, "Not if he is the one doing the biting."

They chuckled, hugged again, and parted.

Her brothers were led away by the overseer and Isabella, and she was left with Sarah and Lekorh.

Remi smiled brightly at them, and they led her out of the building and down to the administration offices where they took an underground shuttle to the VIP quarters.

"It wouldn't be so bad, but I know I could contaminate

the minds of the human women. Learning who I was would flex their grasp of their reality. The boys still look like they are Rrassic."

Sarah cocked her head. "So would you if you resumed your actual appearance."

Of course, they would have picked up on it. "Right. Can we wait until I have some tea or something? I have been practicing holding this look for a while."

Lekorh chuckled. "It is visible on the medical scans. You have the same glands under your hair follicles that a Luthin does, and they were active."

She wrinkled her nose. "Fine. It makes it really easy to play hide and seek. I just wanted the folks at large to simply see a bigger human."

Sarah put her hand on Remi's arm. "We see you. It is just strange because our mind is telling us one thing and our eyes are telling us the other."

Remi nodded, and as they left the shuttle, she let her true skin tones emerge.

Sarah stopped in her tracks and stared. "Wow."

Remi chuckled. "You should see the markings beneath my suit. Please, I really need some tea."

Lekorh eased Sarah away from her, and they entered the lift. His question was casual. "Do your brothers have the same markings?"

"Our whole family does. The boys are wearing the Nool colouring for the sake of orientation. When they are settled, they will let their colouring out."

The lift whisked them to an upper floor. The door opened, and Remi stepped out. "This is beautiful. Is it your home?"

Sarah blinked. "No, it is one of the VIP guestrooms. It is coded to your ident band."

Remi looked down at the band that she had worn all her life. "Ah, right."

She walked through the wide and open expanse and went to the glass doors, triggering the panel that let her out onto the balcony. She looked down and felt her hair being tugged by the wind. She was over a hundred feet up the mountainside, and she felt warm and at home.

Sarah cleared her throat. "Lekorh is making tea. Can I ask, when did the markings show up?"

"I have always had the ones around my eyes. The rest of the markings arrived at puberty." She knew that the black lines that rimmed her eyes and traced around the edge of her lips were different than her mother's even colouring.

The rushes of gold of different colourings accentuated her eyes and cheekbones, running down her neck in darker colouring over her warmer areas. She was a map of exaggerated outlines, and it had a rather pleasing effect overall.

"What about Alia?"

"She is still a child. She has the markings around all of her eyes, but her skin is a determined soft silver." She chuckled.

Sarah smiled, but her mind was on her daughter. She hesitated. "Do you know why she didn't contact me?"

Remi put her arm around Sarah, feeling like an older sibling, not the younger of the two. "I am guessing, but I think she thinks Lekorh is better at math than you are."

Sarah blinked and snorted. "She might be right. Okay. Enough about me. How is your mother doing?"

Remi walked back inside with the human-Saya, and she chuckled. "She has fifteen children of her own in different stages of puberty. She is trying to hold time still and rush it past at the same time."

Lekorh nodded. "The next shift is going to have more couples so that they won't have the same amount of parenting that your mother did."

"Good, because Mom said that the maximum ratio would be one couple to fifteen children. Any more than that and you started to forget names."

Sarah blinked. "Right."

"I stepped in with the younglings, and my parents were able to make sure that the teens and elders had the social niceties."

Lekorh asked, "Can you use invisibility?"

She reached out and took her mug of tea, going invisible while they watched. "What do you think?" She sipped at her tea while the two telepaths stared.

She kept her mind carefully blank and repetitively sipped at her tea.

Sarah reached out and touched her. "I can't even feel you, and I can always feel Luthin."

Remi faded back into view. "I am not Luthin. All of my brothers can do this. Even the two who are manifesting as Zjin and Regiz."

"That is . . . that is unheard of. The other hybrids are localized to their parent genes." Lekorh looked like he wanted to talk to Iktabi.

She smiled. "Feel free to inform the overseer. My other siblings will be here in a few days as well as your daughter. Our genes are compounded, not split, by our nature."

Lekorh got up and went to the com station. He spoke rapidly in High Rrassic and seemed to be concentrating on her physique and testing her siblings to see what they could do.

Remi piped up in High Rrassic, "Just ask them to show off. They will do it immediately."

Lekorh was startled, but he relayed it.

Sarah grinned. "You speak High Rrassic?"

"Of course. My father was very specific that we should be as Rrassic as we could be. There will be no reason for us to be snubbed by the council, other than our hybrid status. If the next generation holds to the Rrassic characteristics, we will rapidly become the new face of the Rrassic."

Sarah blinked. "Holy crap."

"That is what my mom said when Dad laid it out for her. The mating schedule they selected did not account for a monthly cycle and rapid gestation enhanced by the equipment."

Sarah whispered, "Do you have a monthly cycle?"

"Oh, no. It is an annual event for me. Thankfully." She smiled. "I do a lot of training, and the cycle is distracting as hell."

"Tell me about it. I thought that I would have longer in between, but it still comes every thirty days."

Lekorh returned to the table, and he had a sober expression. "The examiner has arrived, and he is being brought here."

Remi was a little surprised. She pointed at the room around her. "Here?"

Sarah shook her head. "No, the upper level is designed for the examiner. He will be able to come and go. From what Lekorh has told me, he has wings."

Remi relaxed. "Oh, okay."

They chatted for a bit, and then, they left her with the Imrahl database.

On her way out, Sarah stopped and said, "I have used the med scans to order clothing for you. I am using a version of our clothing as there is really no position here that matches what you are."

"Thank you, Aunt Sarah. Your care is heartwarming." She bowed low, and Sarah touched her head. There was a tiny flicker of warmth spreading like frost.

When she straightened, Sarah and Lekorh were gone into the lift to their floor above her.

For the first time in her life, she was alone, so she did what anyone would do, she removed her weapons, ran into the bedroom, and jumped on the bed, giggling madly.

She had her own bedroom and her own food dispenser. This was heaven.

CHAPTER THREE

K romir stepped through the portal and fluffed his wings. "Overseer, thank you for greeting me."

The Dorbin-Rrassic inclined his head. "Examiner. Thank you for coming. This species has tremendous potential."

Kromir flexed his wings. "Do you have quarters for me?"

"We do. This is my mate, Isabella. She has made the arrangements."

Kromir looked around, and then, a small female stepped out from behind Iktabi's flared wings.

She snorted. "It would be easier for him to meet me if he could see me."

Iktabi scowled, and despite his exhaustion, Kromir was intrigued. The little female was wearing wrist tethers and had a necklace that matched them. Her hair was up in a businesslike twist, and she was wearing a charming, rich purple dress. Her features were pleasing, and her skin was smooth without any trace of the nap that his people were born with.

"I am pleased to meet you, Examiner Kromir."

He looked at her carefully. "How many children have you spawned?"

"To date? Two." She smiled. "Both with Dorbin-Rrassic characteristics. One is nearly mature at the creche, and the other will be going in his canister this week."

The pride in her tone was startling. Many of the other females of diverse species resented carrying their children but were upset when they were removed for proper education.

It was confusing.

"I hear that even your Saya has found a mate among the samples."

The overseer nodded. "She is very powerful, and their first child is also being raised at our creche."

Kromir blinked. "I was not aware that she could breed a Saya. They told me there was a possibility but not that it had been accomplished."

"Her child has yet to mature or be tested."

He nodded and asked the all-important question. "When will we know?"

"A few days."

"Fine. I will evaluate the others tomorrow." He gave them a sober gaze.

Iktabi's mate nodded. "Your accommodations are ready. If you come with us, we will escort you."

Kromir asked, "Are they keyed to me?"

Iktabi said, "They are. The VIP quarters are accessible from the air. You are on the upper floor. Head for the mountain range, and you will see the structure when you are closer."

Kromir smiled. "Good, it has been too long since I have stretched my wings."

Iktabi inclined his head. "We will call on you in the morning, and you will see the hybrids in action."

Kromir nodded. "Excellent. I look forward to it. Now, show me the exit, and I will be on my way."

He followed the Dorbin-Rrassic and the man's small mate, and he tried to figure out the possible result of such a mating. The hybrids from those two would be small and not what the Rrassic needed. The Voboth were devastating, large, and vicious, and they were getting closer. The Rrassic needed new warriors, and the slight creature next to the overseer could hardly produce a suitable genetic contribution. How they were considered at all was beyond him.

Kromir made it into the soft night of Imrahl, and he inhaled deeply. The air was sweet and warm. It was a good place to spur on courtships but a bad place to train warriors. He bent his knees, pushed upward, and grunted as his wings fought to carry him aloft.

He was too soft from all the administration. He needed to use his body for more than just transport. He wanted to be on the front lines, but they didn't allow his kind there. Mrek-Rrassic were doomed to be judges, assessors, and examiners. They could see what others ignored because they were too attached to their new species.

Kromir pulled himself higher and higher, enjoying the feel of the wind against him and the bright orbital bodies in the sky.

The mountain range was in the distance, and he flew toward it with his wings finally getting the idea that they were not just decorative.

He scanned the ground as he flew and saw the farms that were producing vast quantities of food for the other colonies whose population was not as suited to working the land. The samples they had chosen did have a knack for making the most of their situation.

The mountain complex was interesting. The roof had a wooden floor, an outdoor bathing area, and a door that led back into the mountain. It looked like a very comfortable nest for him to spend a few days in. He fought the urge to appreciate the care that had been taken to make it comfortable.

His gaze dropped to the windows of the floors below, and he was startled at the sight of a female, standing out on a balcony and wearing only a wrap with a cascade of dark gold and black hair blowing around her.

She wasn't a human and wasn't any Rrassic that he had

ever seen before.

Her startled eyes locked with his, and she disappeared.

He banked and lowered himself until he was even with the balcony where he had seen her. There was no sign of her. He blinked and flew upward to his quarters. If she existed, he would see her again, and if he did not, it was probably his urge to see a great Rrassic hybrid taking the stage. He had just never imagined them as females for some reason. They needed warriors, not breeders.

Remi stood with her back to the wall until her senses told her that the male with wings had moved on. She had heard of Mrek-Rrassic when she was learning the nine types with the two uncommon Rrassic being so rare that they were only seen in the councils.

Black feathers. He had golden skin and black feathers. She closed her eyes and calmed her mind. She had thought she was safe to have her shower and walk out for some night air. The Mrek-Rrassic had proved that she was wrong.

Going invisible was a stupid reflex, but she had felt her towel slipping, and she didn't want to be exposed in more ways than one.

She waited until she was sure that he was gone, and then, she kept herself invisible and peeped around the corner. The air was clear.

Remi exhaled softly and tightened her wrap. She resumed her visibility and headed back to her bedroom. There would be time enough to figure out who the creature had been in the morning, but his hot copper eyes had burned into her for a moment before she had hidden. It was like he had seen into her soul in that instant. All she had seen was his Rrassic council uniform and his tremendous wingspan.

She wanted to ask someone about the new arrival, but it

was late, and it was time to get some sleep. Tomorrow, she and her brothers had to prove that their status as hybrid warriors was valuable.

She folded her towel over the back of the chair in her room, and she crawled into bed. When she closed her eyes, she saw the stranger silhouetted against the moons. She quirked her lips and let her thoughts carry her away.

It was a long and restless night, but she got some pleasure out of it.

The next morning, Sarah and Lekorh met her for breakfast before dawn, and Lekorh busied himself in the kitchen while Sarah helped her choose her clothing for the proving ground.

"I am not really good at clothes, but the selection here should suit you. Your father picked them out, and then, your mother vetoed his choices and sent a second request. So, you have both."

Remi grinned, and the choices were obvious. "So, I think I know whose choices I am looking at." She pulled one of the outfits down. "This is my father's choice. He wants me to find a mate."

"How can you tell?"

Remi glanced at her. "Well, as I am not human, I am not under the protections that you all had. I fall under Rrassic membership, or I will after today. Right now, I am nothing. I am a being in between."

Sarah looked at the clothing in confusion.

"Oh, sorry. I went off there. Dad wants me to find a mate, so his clothing selections all show skin. Mom's make me look feminine but warrior-like."

"That is a good way to describe it."

"Well, that is what I am after today. So, sorry, Dad. To-day, I need to be able to move without my breasts on display."

Sarah giggled as Remi removed an outfit that would definitely be more appropriate.

Remi put on the leggings, and then, she pulled on the top, the long tunic fell to her knees and was slit up either side. The sleeves were long, and she could loop her thumb through the edge of the cuff and gain the protection for her wrists.

There were designs embroidered on the tunic, but they were designs of a matching colour, so the fabric was elaborate but still subtle. It was a green so dark that it was almost black, but it was a very comfortable colour for her.

"Let me check something." She went invisible and felt the small barbs in her skin seek out the fabric and act through it.

She walked over to the mirror, and she couldn't see anything. She went visible again, and Sarah blinked at her. "That is . . . wow."

Remi smiled. "My father's legacy. You will see what my brothers can do shortly."

"Great. Breakfast first." Sarah clapped her hands and walked into the kitchen where Lekorh was cooking.

"I was just going to get something through the dispenser."

Lekorh glanced at her, and he chuckled. "I am sorry to disappoint you, but Sarah needs a higher caloric intake than she is willing to engage in, so I sneak it into her food."

Remi chuckled. "In that case, I will set the table."

They chatted and ate swiftly. Sarah did the dishes, and then, they were heading down to the shuttle.

In the capsule, Lekorh asked casually, "Did you see the new arrival last night? The examiner is staying on the roof."

"Ah, he nearly saw me. I think I managed to hide in time. Pretty sure."

Lekorh chuckled. "You will find out today. He will be

watching the proving."

"Great. What will we have to do?"

Sarah stared at her mate. "Yes, what will they have to do?"

"They will have to show us what they can do, in whatever manner they choose."

Remi nodded. "I think I know how to do that. We will need a ball."

Sarah blinked. "A ball?"

"A basketball. We are used to playing rough."

Sarah touched her mind for clarity, and by the time they were walking out of the admin building and heading for the secure Rrassic gym, the ball was on the court.

Remi grinned when she saw her siblings come in under escort, and they were all wearing plain black outfits.

Tomos came up to her. "So, what are we doing?"

"We are showing them what we can do, so I propose a game of basketball."

He smiled. "Can I be on your team?"

"Nope. You pick your two, and I will take the leftover."

"Aw, we make a fair team against three."

She chuckled. "We would slaughter them. Come on, we can use all of our skills. They want us to use all of our skills, and they want to see us for what we are."

He sighed. "Are you sure?"

"This is an assessment. I am sure. This is why we exist. They should know what will be coming through that portal when it opens again."

Tomos nodded. "Fair enough. You can take Arrow."

"Good. Now, we just have to wait for the assessor." She went over to her brothers and explained what they were going to do. The other two were disappointed that Arrow was going to be on her side.

Ari scowled, but Arel said, "I want to be on your team."

Tomos sighed. "Me, too, but she has to go up against someone, and so, we are it."

"I will take it easy on you." She murmured it.

Tomos looked at her in surprise. "You will not. We will play to win, and you will play to win. To do anything else would be disrespectful to our parents."

She nodded. "Right. Well, he has arrived, so we had better get into our places."

Remi and Arrow walked to the edge of the game area. Sarah met her and handed her the tablet that she had asked for in the shuttle.

A few keystrokes brought up the projection of the ball court with the elongated hoop to throw the ball through. She linked it to the arena, and the projection took form.

Sarah blinked at her. "How did you know how to do that?"

"I have grown up with this tech. I was trained to use it."

They waited for the examiner, and when he entered the space, Remi felt like all the air had just left the room.

Arrow whispered, "What is the problem?"

She answered in another whisper. "No problem. I just thought that I dreamed him, but nope, he was up in the sky near my quarters."

Her brother growled. "He was looking at you."

She smiled and elbowed her brother. "Not for long. Now, are you ready?"

He nodded. "I am. No holds barred?"

"Nope, but stay ready to throw me if I need it."

"Aye, aye."

They stood ready and waited for the examiner to take a seat with the overseer and the Saya. It was time to make their family proud.

CHAPTER FOUR

Remi faced her brothers, and she asked, "Do you want the ball, or do we flip for it?"

Ari bent, and he did a standing backflip, landing nearly where he had started.

Remi grinned and gave his team the ball. "Nice flip."

She called out, "Overseer, will you give the order to begin?"

"Begin!"

Ari went forward, and Remi jumped back and to the side, blocking him and getting the ball in her control, slamming it repeatedly onto the ground as she moved. She saw Arrow making his run for the hoop, and when she sensed the other three at her back, she jumped forward, was caught by Arrow's hands, and he flung her up toward the fourteen-foot hoop. She slammed the ball through the hoop and fell to the ground a moment later. The ball dropped a few seconds later, and she tossed it to Tomos.

He gripped the ball, turned, and the chase was on to the other end of the court.

Remi ran full out and went invisible in front of the audience to an audible gasp. Arrow did the same, and with a quick move, she was able to get the ball, throw it to her partner, and he took it back toward their hoop. The other three disappeared, and she regained her appearance as her feet slammed onto the surface of the court. She let out a sharp whistle, and the ball was hurled upward.

Remi sensed that Ari was making a move toward it, so

she swatted his legs and knocked him sideways. Arlen was next to her, and she nudged him to one side, but he moved to block her.

Tomos was behind her, and there was only one thing to do. She stopped, dropped, and Tomos ran over her. She bounded back to her feet as her brothers became visible in their collision, and she got up just in time to watch Arrow catching the descending ball in midair and slamming it into the hoop.

He landed lightly and walked over to her. Touching her cheek. "He stepped on you."

Remi grinned with a wince. "I know. You don't even want to know how big his foot is in comparison with my ribs."

There was a sharp sound, and they turned to the watchers. Remi walked over, and Tomos was next to her. He winced. "Sorry."

"I knew where you were. I will heal."

The examiner walked up to them and looked them over. Remi kept her gaze just beyond his shoulder. She didn't want to look into those copper eyes again.

"So, you are all from the same pairing?" He was standing in front of her. His chest was taking up her entire field of vision.

She looked up, and her body heated. She had no idea why she was acting in such a stupid way, but her body was waking nerves that had been dormant. "We are."

He smiled. "You are the eldest?"

"I am, by two months. This is my eldest brother."

"The other three?"

"All from one collection. We are the first of our parents' twenty."

He nodded. "Right, well as interesting as this display has been, I have set up five projection suites for you to work through. You will all be on your own, and we will see what your instincts lead you to. So, if you will follow me?"

Remi inclined her head, and the others nodded. "Please, lead us."

He paused and then nodded.

Remi and her brothers followed the glossy black feathers as he took them out of the main area, down a hall, a pair of steps, and around a corner.

The guards outside each of the suites gave a hint to the nature of their tests.

"Battle simulations. Ah." Remi nodded. When he stopped in front of the first one, she stepped toward the door.

He shook his head. "I have read your file, this one is not yours."

One by one, her brothers were assigned to their testing chambers. She was finally standing next to the last door, and she raised her brows. "Is this one mine?"

"It is." He raised his voice toward the others. "You can enter your tests now."

As one, all of her brothers went into their chambers, and Remi turned to enter hers.

The examiner held out his arm to bar her. "You do not need to take this test. It is for the warriors."

She nodded and smiled, ducking past his arm. "My mother did not raise anyone who wasn't."

She entered the room before he could stop her, and she closed the door behind her. There was no light, no sound, nothing.

Remi walked forward, and a dim light came on in the distance. A voice murmured, "You are to rescue one of the humans without suffering crippling injury yourself."

Remi nodded, looking around. A scent came to her, and she recognized it as Voboth. She shivered but took another step forward before walking along in a slight crouch, her senses on high alert.

When she heard the screams and shrieks, she stepped up her pace.

The building she was in was made of metal and could have been a spacecraft. The air tasted strange, but she didn't have a basis for comparison.

The light got brighter, and she finally could see the humans. They were gathered in a pit and were shrieking in panic, male and female. The reason for their panic was the partially dismembered corpses pinned and hanging from the upper gallery that overlooked the pit. Bodies from twenty different species were dangling there, and to the side was a Voboth, shouting an ultimatum.

"One of you must become part of our collection. It is up to you to choose. Once we have our prize, we will release the rest of you."

Remi was sickened, but she knew what she had to do. She went invisible, lowered herself over the edge of the gallery and down into the pit. Once there, she used her camouflage to make her into a human woman. She couldn't help her height, but she looked the part.

The humans were shoving at each other. Some were protecting their friends and others were sobbing. Remi stood up straight and raised her hand.

"I will go. I will do it."

Heads turned toward her and confusion rippled through them.

The Voboth nodded, and a metal claw reached down from the ceiling and hooked around her. The claws dug in and lifted her out of the crowd, hoisting her up until she was staring into the pale eyes of the Voboth.

"You would become part of my collection?"

She hung from the claw, the arms of it digging in around her waist until she could barely breathe. "I would."

She was pulled toward it, and the heat rippling off its body had a sickening dampness that made her wince. She held her human seeming.

"We plucked these screaming creatures off their world, and they are wailing like children. What makes you different?"

She glanced over at the crowd, and she paused. She recognized the faces in the panicked throng. Sarah, Lianne, Megan, women that her mother had shown her images of since she had wondered why her parents were different. All of those humans were here.

"I like to look around." She reached out and gripped one of the claws, pushing it back until it snapped. She dropped to the platform in front of the Voboth. "I like to pay attention."

She used the claw as a scythe and embedded it into the Voboth. It didn't put up much of a fight, and that was wrong as well. Killing the Voboth was not the point of the test.

Remi looked around, and the humans were cheering, some were looking at her in shock. Suddenly, a cry came up from the pit. "Take us home!"

The humans in the pit took up the chant, and Remi was left looking for the controls. She had to get them back where they belonged.

The controls were against one wall, and she moved as quickly as she could, unlocking the history of the ship and finding where they had picked up their cargo.

She froze. According to the logs, all the humans had come from the same place. She looked at their position relative to the Earth, and she turned them around. She aimed the ship for the surface of the moon, set the engines at full, and locked the controls.

She stood and watched the ship approach the moon, and when there was no going back, she turned to the humans in the pit.

She leaned over the railing, and she said, "You are going back to your own space."

One of the women smiled and said, "Thank you, hybrid."

She inclined her head, and the ship buried itself in the moon that circled the Earth. Remi stayed with them as the ship collapsed and the impact killed them all.

Remi woke on a med-bed. She cleared her throat. "So, how badly did we fail?"

The assessor was standing at the foot of her bed, and her brothers surrounded her. "You all passed, but you were the only one to identify the complete threat. I would recommend that you use the escape pod the next time you want to crash a ship."

She shrugged. "They were scared; I had to keep them together."

"Well done, Remi Bree-Arix. Your parents are an excellent pairing. You and all of your brethren are fit for duty."

She tried to sit up and winced as she felt a few bruises. "Great."

Tomos frowned. "What was your simulation?"

The assessor quirked his lips. "She was given the same situation as you were. She simply saw more of it than you did."

Tomos chuckled. "Of course, she did. How many did you save?"

The assessor checked his records. "Nine billion."

Her brothers closed their eyes, and Ari opened them with a groan. "They weren't human."

The assessor nodded. "Correct, but you used excellent retrieval tactics. All of you managed to retrieve a minimum of thirty of the beings on the ship, with the exception of Remi. That will qualify you as Hunters in the Rrassic forces."

Remi got herself upright and was thankful that the safeties had triggered in the simulation. She only felt lightly crushed.

Arrow cocked his head. "What about Remi?"

The assessor looked at her with his copper eyes hot. "There are other plans for Remi Bree-Arix."

Remi didn't shiver at his look, but it was only determination that held her still. She really hoped he was referring to her skill as an analytical tracker but had a suspicion that she was going to end up in the Breeder compound. It was hard to keep a bright outlook for her brothers when her heart was sinking at the thought of a fate surrounded by children . . . again.

Running one daycare was enough for a lifetime.

CHAPTER FIVE

She sighed in relief when the medic pushed through the men surrounding her and gave her the pain medication that would help break down the lactic acid in her muscles.

Tomos scowled. "I thought she was treated already."

The assessor scowled. "As did I."

The medic growled. "I was waiting for her to wake up and demand assistance, but she was dealing with you, and that didn't happen. We haven't treated the hybrids yet, and they need to be awake and alert during treatment."

Remi remained still while the drugs did their work and her body moved more rapidly to recovery.

The medic checked the readout, and he nodded. "Good. A little regenerative therapy for the bruising and you will be out of here in six hours."

Ari hissed. "Six?"

The medic nodded. "She took the brunt of the simulator's force. From what I have been told, the computer thought she would move. She didn't. It nearly crushed her before the safeties kicked in."

The assessor scowled. "That is unacceptable. Everyone out. Medic, I will return in a few minutes with a Saya. I would recommend you not be here."

Remi frowned. "If my brothers are not needed elsewhere, I would like them here."

He looked at her, and he raised the small handheld unit that he had. "They are being scheduled for body armor and weaponry fitting."

Her brothers' bands chimed, and she gave the assessor a dark look. "Sneaky."

He shrugged.

One by one, her brothers left the room, and the assessor was the last. "Hey, Assessor."

"It is examiner."

"Fine. Examiner. What is your name?"

He blinked slowly and smiled. "Examiner Kromir."

"Thank you. It is frustrating to not know the name of the person you want to call a jackass." She smiled sweetly, and the medic spluttered next to her.

Kromir's wings snapped tight to his back, and he left her room.

"You shouldn't have said that, but it was funny." The Nool medic grinned.

"I know. But I hate being bossed around. I am the bossiest one in my family."

The medic nodded. "How are you even speaking? You have four broken ribs."

"Practice. Having a lot of brothers means that I play rough. You can't show the pain, but the more I hurt, the snarkier I get."

"You must be in agony because I have never heard of anyone insulting an examiner before." He settled the regeneration lights over the bed, and the radiation spilled into her system, triggering healing.

He left her, and in a few minutes, Kromir returned with Lekorh behind him.

She nodded to Lekorh and glared at Kromir. The Saya was obviously startled that her hostility was written on her features.

"Saya Lekorh, I would like you to examine the mind of this hybrid to determine her state when she knew that the targets were false in the simulation."

Lekorh nodded, and Remi let him touch her thoughts and winced when he staggered back.

Kromir looked at him with concern. "What is wrong?"

"She is in incredible pain."

"What?"

"Her ribs are broken, she has bruises down her spine and back. There is intense pain around her scalp, and one of her hands is swollen, her knuckles are damaged."

Remi looked at her left hand, and he was right. It was purple.

Kromir stared at her and asked Lekorh, "Can you get past the pain?"

Remi smiled. "I will pull it aside for you."

She tamped it down and sat there while Lekorh went through her mind.

"She determined that she was going to die with those who could not live because if she left, they would panic, and there was a chance they could make it off the ship."

Kromir nodded. "Is she aware that one of her kind is not asked to self-sacrifice?"

Lekorh asked the question she was thinking. "A hybrid?"

"A female."

She rolled her eyes and felt the laughter in her mind contributed by Lekorh.

"My sex does not restrict my capabilities or my responsibilities to my society and the purpose of the Rrassic. I was not born because I am female, I was born because my parents created me. No matter what sex I am, I would still be here. My purpose was decided before my body shape was known."

Kromir blinked slowly. He sighed, and she watched the movement of his chest as he breathed deeply. The suit he was wearing wasn't quite tight enough for her taste.

Lekorh gave her a shocked look, and she shrugged slightly. Hormones would be hormones, even if the target of her lust were looking at her with a suspicious glare.

"What was that? What passed between you?"

Lekorh paused. "I do not feel it is in my purview to tell you, Examiner."

Remi sighed. "Just so he doesn't get into trouble, my biological systems are coming online, and my hormones seem to be fascinated by you."

Kromir took a step back. "What?"

The whisper was as close to a shout as she imagined he could manage.

"Don't worry. I am sure it will fade." She waved it off with her right hand. The left was the focus of the healing rays.

"Unacceptable." He stepped toward her, and then, he paused and stepped back before he turned and stalked out of the room.

Lekorh turned back to her, and he grinned. "The attraction is mutual, but he has no idea what to do about it."

She grinned. "I have a few ideas, but the wings add a bit of a challenge to some of the moves."

He put his hands over his ears. "I am not listening."

She laughed, winced at the pain, and lay back. "I am just going to lie here until the light is finished with me. After that, I will head to my quarters to get some rest."

"You aren't going to worry about your brothers?"

"Of course, I am. I will worry about all my siblings, but it doesn't stop the fact that we are at war. We were designed for war, and our parents were brought together because of a war. If we fight and win, we will have to find our place in the universe because we have only been born to Imrahl, and it is a flicker in the hour of the universe."

Lekorh was surprised. "How do you know that? Even Sarah doesn't know that."

"The logic doesn't fit. Why would they have us born and raised at high speed and then step us directly into a situation where time was passing at the same time as Imrahl. Imrahl is a creche of another sort. It is a place to hide an army, and we are willing to become that army."

"You must keep that knowledge to yourself."

"Only if you answer this one thing for me."

He looked around and then nodded. "Fine. What?"

"How long will have passed from when the initial humans were sampled in the human world until now?"

He nodded. "Right. About twenty days. We are looking to stage for the defense of Earth in another two months of their time. The Voboth will be arriving in Earth space in four months, Terran time."

She nodded. "Right. So, we will be ready when that happens."

"Or your children will be."

"Who am I cleared to mate with? Rrassic? Other hybrids? I don't know if there are any rules that guide me."

"That will be determined by the examiner."

She smiled. "Thank you. I will head back to the VIP quarters the moment that I am released from medical."

"Good. I will see you this evening. We will bring you something for dinner."

Remi chuckled. "Please make it junk food. I was just going to molest the food dispenser for stuff that I wasn't able to get in the creche."

He inclined his head. "I will see what I can do. Rest and heal."

She nodded and relaxed in the bed, letting the regenerating light work its stimulation on her cells. She had some time to kill, so she ran fantasies of Kromir through her thoughts. Nothing would come of it, but she really wished it could.

A light touch on her forehead and cheek woke her. She didn't open her eyes, but the soft caress moved to her lips, tracing them lightly.

She waited until the finger withdrew before she opened her eyes and looked at her companion. "Examiner. I thought you had left."

"I returned. Your skin is fascinating. You truly looked like a human in the simulation."

Remi smiled slightly. "Just the follicles on the surface of my skin, like any Luthin."

"But you are not a Luthin, and though your brothers presented themselves to this world as Nool, none of them are. They all became their Rrassic designations far earlier than one of us. That was not common knowledge."

She shook her head lightly. "We thought it best that it was discovered more organically than having them all troop through the portal in their mature forms."

"But they all have Luthin characteristics as well."

Remi shrugged. "My dad's genes carried through. All of his children are Luthin to some extent."

"How many sisters do you have?"

"Eight in total. Eleven brothers."

He exhaled. "Are they all accelerators?"

"As far as our testing indicates, yes." She checked the display to see the progress on her healing. She still had ten minutes to go. Most of her body was fine; it was her hand that was getting all the attention.

He nodded. "Tell me about the other hybrids from the other matches."

She sat and told him about the Zjin, Regiz, and Dorbin-Rrassic children. So far, the fathers' genetics were breeding true, but the children were exhibiting traits of other Rrassic clans as well.

"How are their developments?"

"Behind my family by a decade, but once we even out with medical assistance, they catch up in short order."

"How old are you, in simple years you have lived."

"By Rrassic standards, I am forty years old. My lifespan is estimated around five hundred years if there is nothing to interfere with it."

Kromir nodded. "I see. I would like to speak with you about it later. Perhaps over dinner?"

"Ah, Lekorh and Sarah are bringing over dinner while I rest from the breaks and bruises."

"Excellent. I will accompany them, and we can share a meal."

Remi couldn't argue with him, so she smiled weakly. "Let them know, and I will see you there."

He smiled, and to her shock, he leaned over and pressed a kiss to her lips. The kiss was slow, warm, and exploratory. When he leaned back, he licked his lips. His smile was wicked. "I will definitely see you tonight."

She looked at the time ticking down on the display, and she wanted it to accelerate already.

Remi was going to have to wait until she was healed, and then, she could go back to her quarters and work out what she was going to wear to a business-casual meal with a man she respected. The nervousness caused fear in her; she wasn't used to fearing. She had been raised to be a woman who could take action, not wait and see. Now, she was stuck waiting and losing patience rapidly.

It was quite the high wire to walk.

CHAPTER SIX

Remi sat down in the shuttle and waited for the few minutes that it sent her under the surface of Imrahl and back to her quarters.

She brushed her fingers over her lips, remembering the kiss. It might have been her first proper kiss, but he had either studied or practiced a bit. Remi shook off her daze when the transport stopped, and she headed for the lift. She was too old to be mooning around like this, or so her mother would say. Her body had left puberty behind almost two decades ago. It was ridiculous for her to be so focused on Kromir. He was going to bring his report back to the Rrassic council, and she would never see him again.

Remi chuckled and thought about the benefits of a short-term relationship. If she did get Kromir into bed and it resulted in a pregnancy, she could start on her way to her allotment of embryos. Having sex with him might not be the worst way to spend an evening.

The lift chimed again. She had been mulling over the idea of a casual encounter so intently, she had missed arriving at her floor. Shaking her head, she stepped into her quarters and looked around. The next day, the rest of her family arrived, and she was not looking forward to sharing space with her eight sisters.

Chuckling, she went to take a shower. Setting the water to cold was supposed to be good for an overheated imagination, so she stood under the punishing spray until her body's heat started fighting back.

She turned off the shower and dried off, seeking out a robe before she went to the balcony. Staring off into the light of her true homeworld, she tried not to think of the fight that she had been created for.

A cool whisper ran through her thoughts, and she blinked. She had been staring out until sundown, and her guests were on their way.

She requested five minutes, and she got a soft laugh through her thoughts.

Moving as quickly as her sore body could, she pulled out a dress that simply slipped over her head. No undergarments were needed or required. She made a face at the light bruising that was still visible on her skin but stepped into sandals and went to answer her door.

Kromir was in the lift, and he blinked in surprise as she stepped aside with a smile.

"Please, be welcome, Examiner Kromir."

He entered her quarters and stared at her. "You appear to be completely healed."

She grinned. The lift closed, and it went to retrieve Lekorh and Sarah.

"Please, come in. Lekorh is going to be doing the cooking. He and Sarah are on their way."

"An actual fresh meal? This is a rare treat." Kromir paused, and his wings expanded slightly to frame his body and the gold and black of his uniform. He looked splendid.

She chuckled. "Can I get you a beverage from the dispenser?"

"Wine if you have it, water if you don't."

She excused herself to let Lekorh and Sarah in. They had full access, her authorization was just a formality.

She welcomed them and asked them about their beverage choices.

Sarah smiled and sat close to her on one of the couches.

"So, how are you feeling after your test?"

Kromir sat on the nearby backless hassock, and he listened in. Remi glanced at Lekorh, but he was busy humming and chopping the raw ingredients for dinner.

"I am fine. I feel a little foolish for getting lost in the moment, but it seemed so real at the time."

"I mean your body and mind. How are you feeling?" Sarah gave her an encouraging nod.

"I am sore but healed. My mind keeps replaying the images of the women screaming for help. That was one of the things that gave it away. I know why the Rrassic took only women, but the Voboth would have had no reason to do that. There was also no way that they could have picked out all the genetic donors so precisely. The entire crowd was wrong."

"How did that make you feel?"

"Disoriented, angry, and upset." Remi paused. "Is this a therapy session?"

"No. Is there anything else going on?"

"Oh, you mean the other thing? Yes, that is still going on. I am not insane yet, but I will need to take action sooner rather than later."

Kromir frowned. "What are you talking about?"

Sarah turned to him with a bland smile. "She is in heat, in case it missed your keen senses."

He jerked upright and stared at Remi. "How are you still sitting there so calmly?"

That was surprising. "What?"

"Rrassic females take dozens of lovers as their heat progresses. They can't be sated. Has it only just begun?"

She shook her head. "No, it has been ongoing for the last ten days or so. And I am a hybrid. I have considerable control over my actions, if not my impulses."

"What is the difference?"

She quirked her lips. "I am neither in your lap right now, nor going to one of the socials to find a mate."

He blinked, and the flames flared in his eyes. "That is an interesting offer."

"It wasn't an offer, it is an impulse. I have control over my actions; therefore, I am having dinner with family friends and a visiting dignitary."

He swallowed slowly. "I see."

Sarah was sitting with her hand over her mouth in amused glee. "We were warned that some of the hybrids might come through in this condition, so we were asked to keep an eye on her."

"Or to mind me, as it were." Remi smiled.

The sizzle and smell of dinner got her attention. "Please, excuse me."

She got to her feet and walked into the kitchen. "Lekorh, do you need assistance?"

He grinned and stepped away from the heating element and the pan. She moved into the evacuated position and tossed the contents expertly. "All of us were taught to cook. Some of us were more enthusiastic than others."

He chuckled. "Excellent. I can't get Sarah to assist unless it is under duress."

They stood, and he added the right vegetable at the right interval until they had enough food to feed ten humans or two Rrassic, a hybrid, and a human.

She set the food out on the low table. Sarah had put the plates and eating prongs in place. They all had their beverages with them as they sat on cushions, and Kromir looked relieved to have enough room to spread his wings out behind him.

"Thank you, Lekorh, for preparing everything." She scooted her dress in a comfortable position.

Lekorh inclined his head. "Thank you for allowing us to

see the real you. Your colouring is really stunning."

"A bit of that is bruising." She inclined her head. "Let's eat."

Kromir was the first one to the main dish, and he smiled as he chewed the first bite. When he swallowed, he said, "I know that the food from the dispenser is healthy, but it doesn't taste nearly as nice as fresh."

Sarah and Lekorh were busy eating.

Remi muttered, "At the creche, all we got was fresh. The dispensers were saved for emergency food for a growth spurt. Everything we are eating here is grown on Imrahl."

Kromir was busy stuffing his face. He looked up and gave her a slight smile.

Remi sighed and tucked into dinner. There was nothing but chewing sounds for several minutes as the feast dwindled to nothing. She wished there was dessert, but she would wait until she was alone and then get some out of the dispenser.

She was about to collect the empty plates, but Sarah got to her feet and whisked everything to the kitchen where she washed the dishes.

Lekorh grinned. "At least the dishes are always taken care of. Sarah's skill at tidying is astonishing."

Sarah called out, "I can hear you."

Kromir looked at them, and his gaze fixed on the grinning Saya. "Lekorh, I must say that I have never met one of your kind who is so relaxed and filled with good humour."

Sarah snickered from the kitchen. "He gets laid. A lot."

Lekorh chuckled. "Occasionally it is even physical."

Kromir was intrigued. "You are also the first Saya I have seen with a drive to mate. How did that come about?"

"I met Sarah. Her mind and mine met and meshed as if they were one. It has been a blissful few weeks with her, and I look forward to decades or centuries more."

Remi smiled. It was apparently a common sentiment with the humans and their mates. Once a Rrassic found the right female and she acknowledged that he was the one for her, a deep sense of anticipation and contentment filled them. Her father was the perfect example of a content Rrassic, and her mother never let him forget it. Only the ability of a Luthin to disappear from view kept things new. Hide and seek was one of the games that her parents still played, four decades into their bonding. No one played hide and seek like a Luthin.

Kromir looked at her. "You are smiling."

"I was thinking of my parents and how they are doing after four decades of union. Human women are remarkably tolerant." She chuckled.

Sarah called out, "Yes, we are."

Remi laughed and sipped at her favourite concoction. She had been so delighted to figure out how to make the creche cocktail in the dispenser that she made it whenever she had the chance. The lightly flavoured water with a hint of fruit juice was always pleasant to consume.

Kromir was drinking wine, and Lekorh and Sarah were drinking water. They couldn't afford to lose control, so non-alcoholic consumables were necessary.

Kromir inclined his head to Lekorh. "Thank you for the meal. It was delightful."

"You are most welcome. I cook all of our evening and morning meals, so while you are here, it would be no trouble to increase the amount if you like."

"I would love to agree, but I will be keeping irregular hours. The reports must be as detailed as I can make them."

Lekorh nodded. "I understand."

The sunset had long faded, and the stars were coming out to blink and shimmer in the sky.

Remi looked over her shoulder, and she tried not to think

about the sky that she wanted to learn firsthand. She wanted to be up and out in those stars and not sitting here and waiting to find out whom she was going to be allowed to breed with.

She wanted a hybrid charter of rights, but that wasn't going to happen. The hybrids were firmly in between being cloned humans and Rrassic citizens. They had no status; they were simply the desired result.

Remi shook her head. She had to stop thinking about that situation. It was pressing on her, but that wasn't what she was here for. Her entire existence was a simple proof of concept, and she had to impress the examiner with the usefulness of her genetics.

She looked over at the examiner in question, and he was having a conversation in High Rrassic about the likelihood that Remi was actually in heat.

She got up and took her cup out onto the balcony, staring out at the night sky. Keeping herself under control was second nature. There were no authorized mates for her in the creche, and as she thought of all of them as little brothers, it was better that way. There was less chance for incidences when you considered all those of a similar species to be related to you.

"You are staring at the stars as if you would pull them down to you." Kromir's voice came from behind her.

She sipped at her cup and kept her gaze at the arch of the sky. "I would pull myself to them if I could."

"Why?"

She turned and leaned against the railing, looking him in the eyes. "What is my life here?"

He paused. "What?"

"What will my life here be? Will I find a mate or one of them after another? Am I to be a breeder, a freak, an example? What about the women who will emerge from the creche behind me? What will their role be?"

"It has not yet been decided. They are waiting until my report is issued."

She tapped her fingers on the cup. "What is your current inclination?"

"To bend you back over that railing and kiss you until your head spins then fly you up to my quarters where we can share a discussion and a bath in the deep tub."

She smiled and pressed her cup to her forehead. "I meant for the hybrid women?"

He grinned. "Ah, that. You have demonstrated battlefield intelligence, analytical skills that surpassed your brethren, and awareness of the situation to get the threat neutralized. I am recommending any comparable females for command positions."

"Put that in writing."

He shrugged. "I already have. My preliminary report has been forwarded to the council. The hybrids of Imrahl are authorized for duty as soon as a sufficient number have been assembled."

Remi leaned down to put her cup next to her feet. "I believe that you mentioned having an inclination?"

He grinned and stepped forward pressing his lips to hers as he wrapped his arms around her.

His inclination was one that she was definitely sharing. She wove her fingers through his hair and hung on while her senses spun out of her control.

CHAPTER SEVEN

Remi kept control of herself until she was sure that Lekorh and Sarah were not in her quarters anymore. She didn't often use her echolocation, but this was one of those times.

Kromir raised his head. "What was that?"

His hands were still firmly gripping her, and she smiled up at him. "Just making sure we are alone."

"But *what* was it?"

"Echolocation. I can use it in short bursts."

"It wasn't on your med reports."

"I wasn't using it then. Using in public spaces is awkward. I don't use it often, and it is tricky to figure out."

"I need to make a note of it." He released her.

She carefully buckled her self-control back into place with a sigh. "Fine."

Remi was resigned to waiting until a more suitable or, at least, focused candidate came her way. Her mind might want Kromir, but her body was going to have to wait.

She leaned down to pick up her cup and walked back to the dispenser for a refill. She was defeated. "What would you like to know?"

"What is the range?" He was following her slowly.

"Three hundred metres. I can't pull it in, so I am getting all the data whether I want it or not." She sipped at her cocktail and turned to find him directly behind her, his body a warm wall that smelled delicious.

"You didn't know I was here."

"No, I reeled in my senses. It gets weird with people around. They keep moving, and I keep tracking them. It gives me a headache."

"Did you use it during the simulation?"

"No. Projections hurt a bit."

"But you have the tool at your disposal." He was frowning.

She sipped at her cup. "Yes. It is very handy underwater."

He sniffed. "What are you drinking?"

She chuckled. "Creche cocktail. Four types of juice liberally diluted with water."

"May I try it?"

She was turning toward the dispenser when he simply gripped her cup and the hand that held it and lifted it to his lips.

She swallowed when he did.

His brows rose high. "That is . . . extremely pleasant."

She chuckled. "Can I have my hand back?"

He smiled. "No."

He took another sip from the same spot she had been drinking, and then, he returned the cup and her hand to her. "I would not have thought that something so simple would taste so complex."

"The key is the dilution to allow the flavours to separate. Without watering it down, it is sickly sweet and very acidic."

He nodded with a slow smile.

She licked her lips quickly. "Is that going in a report as well?"

He leaned down and kissed her softly, running his tongue along the same path hers had taken. "Only if it is necessary."

Remi's body was rioting. She didn't know whether she should be on her guard or up against him.

She leaned back. "What are you doing?"

He stepped forward, and she moved the mug to the countertop.

"Kromir, you seem a little easy to distract, so I would not want to get in the way with you and your pursuit of duty."

He paused. "Do you not want me?"

Honesty was the best policy. "Yes, I do, but as this will be my first encounter of this nature, I need to trust that the person I am with will take appropriate care of me."

He cocked his head. "I agree to your terms."

She didn't squeak when he picked her up. She prided herself on the fact that she didn't squeak. He walked through her quarters and onto the balcony. His wings flared wide, and he stepped up onto the railing.

His fingers wrapped around her bicep and knees as he dropped forward and launched them into the night.

His wings were silent as the steady beats carried them up above the VIP quarters. She looked out over the expanse of Imrahl, and she noted something that wasn't on any of the maps she had memorized as a child. There was another city in the distance.

"What is that?"

He had been banking to land on the deck, and when she asked, he changed direction. "Would you like to see it?"

"Yes, please."

His wings carried them across long kilometres in only a few beats. He was fast.

She breathed in and out through her nose as the wind restricted her lungs' ability to get oxygen.

Remi looked out over the landscape as the low and wide second city took shape beneath her. "Training centres, quarters, running tracks, confidence courses. This is a city for the hybrids."

He chuckled. "Correct. When the population is sufficient for a division to be created, they will move out from this point. There is even a direct portal for troop transport."

"I had no idea. My mother never mentioned it."

"She wouldn't have known. Like the creche, the new city was built in a dimensional bubble. No one would have seen it rising. The construction was designed to remain flat and low so as not to be visible through the treeline."

"Wow. So, only the overseer is aware of it?"

"No. The Saya was also aware of it. Lekorh has skills in temporal communication and was able to keep everyone apprised of the progress."

She smiled. That explained his daughter's skill.

"Something amuses you?"

"Yes, but it can wait until tomorrow to share it." She chuckled.

He did a slow pass over the new city, and then, he beat his wings back toward the VIP building.

"At least my brothers will have somewhere to go."

"Why did they hide their true natures?"

She chuckled and spoke against his neck. "My parents warned us that our full skills might be seen as threatening if they were all revealed at once. A gradual exposure was much easier for everyone concerned."

"So, have I seen all your secrets?" He landed on the deck and walked with her still in his arms.

She shrugged. "Most of them. I haven't been keeping track."

Kromir chuckled. "You are exceptionally impressive, as you are no doubt aware."

Remi wrinkled her nose and felt a stuttering flutter in her chest as he carried her to the bedroom.

He released her legs slowly and turned her to face him. "So, any second thoughts?"

"I am on the ninety-fifth thought if that makes any difference." She smiled and ran her hands up his chest, enjoying the feel of his heart beating faster.

"At least I have been on your mind." He smiled and kissed her, starting with light pressure before their tongues tangled.

She leaned into him and sought out the closure on his uniform. Peeling the tough fabric away from his skin took too much concentration. She wanted to focus on the kiss, but she wanted him naked. Choices, choices.

Remi leaned back, and she tugged at his uniform. "Clothing. Off."

He moved so quickly she only saw a blur of his skin, hair, and eye colour. His wings were flexed to frame his body, and she had to admire the display.

His voice was a low rumble. "Your turn."

She smiled and crossed her arms, gripping her dress below her hips. She pulled the fabric up deliberately until she flipped it over her head and let it slither to the floor. Stepping out of her sandals was an afterthought.

She stood facing him, and she cocked her head. "I can't really match your display."

His eyes blazed, and his erection dipped and wept. "You don't need to match it, you have surpassed it."

She didn't glance down, but she wanted to. It was a weird feeling when you wanted to check your own skin because someone else was staring at it.

They stood for a moment, and her nerve began to buckle. She started to turn away, but he moved swiftly to grip her shoulders.

Remi met his gaze warily.

"It takes getting used to, but you are safe with me."

She smiled slightly. "I have found myself to be safest alone."

"This is not something that one can satisfactorily do alone." He stroked her neck.

She snickered. "I beg to differ."

"This will be different. Trust yourself. I give my body to you freely."

She blinked and nodded. "I give my body to you freely."

Consent was spoken, and she decided to take him at his word.

Touching a Rrassic was not quite like caressing her own skin. Her skin was smooth with a nap so fine it was almost invisible. His skin had a velvety covering that showed the trail of her fingers as she caressed his chest.

He didn't remain still; Kromir stroked his hands over her back, and he cupped her hips, reducing the distance between them.

His cock was pressed against her belly, and Remi now moved her hands slowly over his torso, caressing down to wrap one hand around his erection, slowly pumping until his shaft was slick with his own enthusiastic response.

Kromir shuddered at her slow motions, and he cautiously removed her hand from his erection before lifting her against him and carrying her to the enormous expanse of the bed.

He pressed her carefully to the bed, and he decided to explore. He began with the markings around her eyes, feathering kisses over them before following the darker and lighter pigmentation on her skin with intense focus.

She had no idea that another person's mouth could heighten the riot of her senses. When his tongue moved across her flesh, she gasped and trembled. Her breasts were especially sensitive; the jabbing heat as he sucked and nibbled sent shards of excited lightning to her clit.

After he massaged, licked, and sucked at her breasts, he moved down her belly with long, slow strokes of his tongue.

She shivered when he parted her legs and draped her thighs over his shoulder. The word vulnerable didn't even begin to cover how she felt when his breath moved across her slick folds.

His mouth blazed a trail as he lapped upward with a long drag of his tongue.

Remi clenched the sheets with one hand and covered her mouth with the other. Keeping her sounds to herself was something she had been doing for the last decade. The walls in the creche dorms were a little thin.

When he began to flick her clit with slow strokes of his tongue, she let out a squeak. Her thighs flexed and gripped his head. Her feet were pinned between his wings and his shoulders, and she was stuck as her body started to buck and twist with every wet stroke.

She made a fist and bit the edge of it as his attention took her to the edge of control. When her limbs and belly were coated in a fine sheen of sweat and Kromir showed no sign of stopping, Remi couldn't take it anymore. She stopped muffling herself and shrieked as her body bucked and shivered in his embrace.

Light flared in her vision, her eyes went blind for just a moment, and when the fireworks faded, she was breathing heavily and Kromir had moved into a more comfortable position on top of her.

He licked his lips slowly, and his eyes were blazing when he fitted himself into her wet and welcoming folds.

He slid into her slowly, inch by inch, thrusting and retreating until he was inside her all the way and his body was shuddering to try and keep his own excitement under his control.

Remi wrapped her limbs around him and moved with him, rocking and lifting her hips to meet his thrusts and calculating how long it would take her to reach the peak she had just visited. She wanted to do it again, and she wanted him with her when she vocalized her pleasure. That was one secret that she hadn't parted with . . . yet.

CHAPTER EIGHT

Lying under him, coated with sweat, Remi sighed softly. Kromir had his head pressed into the mattress next to her, his wings were wide and giving them a private space in the huge room.

He was still inside her and still hard. Remi chuckled and ran her fingers through his hair.

Kromir's expression was dazed when he lifted his head. "What did you do to me?"

There was satisfaction in his tone, so she didn't take offense.

"Nothing that you didn't do to me. It was a very satisfying first time. Thank you." She leaned up and kissed him.

He rose up on his elbows and continued the kiss, moving slowly inside her again.

She smiled and wrapped her legs around him again, pulling herself up to him as he rocked in and out of her at a slow and leisurely pace.

He slid an arm under her and shifted, pulling her up against him as he rocked his hips into her. She pressed the soles of her feet together and held onto his shoulders as she looked into his eyes.

Kromir kissed her, holding her head with one hand while the other pulled her rhythmically against him as he thrust.

They rose and fell together with the heat growing slowly between them until the beat of their bodies took on a savagery that left them biting at each other, nipping at lips, and Remi bit the heavy bulk of his shoulder.

She felt the searing bite on her own shoulder, and her body bucked against him, her inner muscles stroking him and triggering his sudden shove into her as his body shuddered.

They locked together, twitching and shaking in alternating spasms. Remi finally withdrew her teeth and waited until he did the same.

It took a long wait of twenty seconds, but he released her, and she could smell her blood in the air. She leaned forward and pressed her forehead against his chest, unwilling to look him in the eye.

He was slowly stroking her back, and she heard wordless murmuring against her head. It was as if he was calming a child.

She smiled against his skin and rubbed her cheek against him.

When he spoke, he summed it up, "That was unexpected."

She chuckled. "I think that is a correct assessment."

He simply held her for a few minutes, and she finally murmured, "I think a soak in that tub would be a good idea before I get stuck like this."

He growled lightly. "I like you right here."

"Try and walk into the council with me jammed on your cock and I will punch you."

She raked her nails down his chest and across his ribs. He twitched. She chuckled. It was nice that he was ticklish.

"Well, if I am under threat, I believe that the tub has a certain appeal."

He moved, walking awkwardly on his knees until he was off the bed.

"You know I can walk."

Kromir let out a happy sigh. "I know, but I love the feel of you wrapped around me, so I believe that I will savour that as long as I can."

He walked out onto the deck, and the fresh air of the evening brought her vividly awake. She couldn't see where they were going, but when he hopped slightly, she held her breath as they dropped and the warm water closed over them.

The water stopped at her collarbone. She smiled and separated from him, the heat from his body missed for a moment before she settled in the water and sought out a bench on the side. She quickly dipped herself to equalize her temperature, and then, she pulled her hair back and twisted it into a long knot that kept it from floating around her.

Kromir disappeared under the water, and he came up, wings first, throwing water everywhere. His wings flapped and threw water off, and he was grinning at her expression.

"You look perturbed."

She cocked her head. "I have seen images from Earth. You look like a black swan."

He took the seat next to her, and his wings flexed and lay flat behind him.

She winced. "Doesn't that hurt?"

"I have ligament attachments for it." He grinned. Kromir sighed. "Now, what am I going to do with you?"

Remi blinked. "I didn't realize that I was yours to worry about."

"All of the people of Imrahl are under my purview as the examiner, but you are the first of your kind. That would normally need a change of venue."

"What?"

"The alien races that we have partnered with have all given us representatives to serve the interests of their people. The hybrids have the potential to reach a population of six hundred thousand. That means they need a voice on the council to represent their interests."

She blinked slowly. "I am not a politician."

"Nor would you be expected to be. You would be a voice for the human-Rrassic hybrids and in communication with your people on Imrahl." He had a calculating look in his eyes. "I think that might be the best plan for you."

Remi was surprised. "Leave Imrahl?"

"All of the hybrids will leave eventually. You have been bred to defend two species, and from what I have already seen, you are a capable commander."

She blushed. "It is easy to boss my brothers around."

"I do not think that is the case, and you are aware of it."

Remi nodded. "Fine. Yes. I can control most of the hybrids, or they will follow me. Either way, it is the same effect. They do what I tell them."

"I guessed as much." His lips quirked. "Once you announced you were interested in me, I knew I had to follow your order."

"I am sure that was your motivation." She splashed him.

"I am altruistic to the core." He snagged her and pulled her into place on his lap.

She scowled but settled. "So, why do you make these decisions?"

"I first examine the new species, and then, I assess them. The hybrids of Imrahl have my admiration and the acceptance of the council. As a blended species, you are strong, intelligent, and aware of what is at stake in this matter."

Part of Remi relaxed. That was a worry off her shoulders and that of her parents. Proving the worth of the hybrids had been a stressful point.

She yawned and settled against him as if all the stress of the last few days had just melted away.

"Tired of me already?"

"It has been a stressful few days. Knowing that the hybrids are suitable for their purpose is a relief."

He seemed surprised. "You were worried?"

"I was. I know what we can do, but trying to prove it to someone else that we are a blend and mutation that can be more than the sum of our species. It is important to me."

He nodded. "The Rrassic have tried to gain allies and troops from a dozen species. The hybrid program was a grasp at getting the help that we need from within the target races."

"So, there are other species on other worlds going through this same process?"

"Yes, but with every round of copies for the original mother species, we got better at integrating our own genes until the humans were generated."

"Why not just clone your entire army?"

"We do not know how long this war is going to rage. It has not even begun to take the toll that it will. Making the same troops over and over will not gain us an advantage. We needed the uncertainty that is brought on by random genetic lottery."

"Basic biology. The ones who are attracted to each other tend to be more genetically favourable." She thought of her parents and how cute they were when her mother was trying to outwit her father. He liked to track his mate, and she liked to get lost; it was an adorable mix.

"What are you thinking of?"

She blinked and chuckled. "My parents. They are a very good mix and were excellent guardians for the other children. I hope the next set of parents on duty do half as good a job."

"The overseer has assigned four of the couples to watch over the development and training for the next batch of embryos."

"Four? Then, there are more couples than I know about."

He chuckled. "There have been a dozen males finding

their mates this week alone. It was a slow start, but more and more of the females are becoming receptive, and the males are learning how to court their mates."

"My father mentioned that dealing with human females was tricky." She smiled. "Then, my mother smacked him on the arm and said that Rrassic males only wanted mates so they could get better quarters."

He curled his arms around her. "What did he say to that?"

"That was usually his cue to pick her up and carry her to their better quarters."

"It was a game?"

"It was a way of stopping an argument. It worked very well." She smiled. "I can hardly wait to see them."

"You have great affection for them." It wasn't a question.

"I do. They made sure that I knew how I came into the world and that tests showed I carried my mom's accelerator genes."

"So, when you are receptive, your children will be in the next round to go to the creche."

"Eventually. I don't even know what the hybrids are allowed to breed with yet."

He went still. "I had not thought of that. None of the other species mature as rapidly as humans, even with the creches. It has not come up yet."

"Ah. Well, I am sure I will be fine."

He leaned in and nuzzled her ear. "You don't believe that we managed to start something tonight?"

She blinked slowly. "Honestly, that had not occurred to me. I forget that that is the purpose of all the wild hormones and distracting fantasies."

"Fantasies? Do tell."

"Well, they mostly involve working around the wings. I was under the misapprehension that they were not as flexible as they obviously are."

He grinned. "Oh, they are very flexible."

"Good. Most of my sex fantasies involve me on top, so as long as you are here, it is good to know that we are on the same page."

He laughed and nipped at her ear. "It is a very good thing. I look forward to assisting in your fantasies' transformations to reality."

She grinned and sat in the hot water with him until the moon was high in the sky. When she felt him tense to move, she clambered off his lap and scrambled to the edge of the tub, flexing her legs and enjoying being on her own two feet again.

"You object to my carrying you?" He got out of the water with a whoosh.

"No, but I have perfectly sound limbs, and I like to use them." She bent, stretched, and flexed while he watched.

"I can see that. Are you done showing off?"

She had been bending over to stretch her inner thighs. "I believe so."

"Good. Stretch later."

He caught her around the waist and carried her back into the bedroom where the bots had tidied the bed. He set her down next to the bed, and then, he flopped on his back, his wings easing his transition from vertical to horizontal.

His smile was genuine. "I am all yours."

She rubbed her hands together and tried to decide where to start. There was just so much muscled goodness, she may as well start in the middle and work her way out. She climbed onto him and started working her fantasy into reality. Exploring new territory was definitely a fun occupation.

CHAPTER NINE

The chime at the door brought her head up. She was curled up on Kromir's wing and effectively pinning him down.

He was grinning. "So, you forgot about breakfast?"

She was very glad for her pigmentation because it didn't show the heat that her face was broadcasting. With care, she got off his wing and looked for her dress from the previous night.

"Do not worry. They are Saya. They already know."

She shot him a dark look.

The dress was hanging in the wardrobe next to his uniforms.

"I am going to my quarters for a fast shower and a change of clothing."

He grinned. "As you like. Please, let Sarah and Lekorh in."

She stalked over to the door and smiled at the telepaths. "Hello, I will return in a moment."

Sarah was smiling. "Take your time, dear. Breakfast will be ready when you return."

Lekorh looked a little less casual. "It will give us a moment to discuss things with Kromir."

Remi was in the lift when she recognized the expression on Lekorh's face. He was filled with fatherly outrage. She had only seen the expression once before when one of the Nool that was there as a manufacturer had developed into a Regiz, and he had a fascination for her. Her father and brothers had shown him that he was outnumbered and not able to pursue her. When he tried anyway, Remi had kicked his ass, but she recognized the expression on the Saya's features. He wanted to protect her. How sweet.

She took a quick shower and pulled on one of the tunic and legging combinations with boots. She was comfortable, she had ease of movement, and her hair was in a thick braid down her back. There was nothing sexy about her.

She got back in the lift and returned to Kromir's quarters. Lekorh and Kromir were not in the room, and Sarah was shredding cheese.

"Can you cook?" Sarah looked a little desperate.

"I can. Omelettes?"

"Yes. Please. The boys are still talking."

Remi got to work and was soon folding one omelette after another, all with different fillings, onto platters. Sarah was excellent at prep work.

They transferred all the food to the table along with tea and water. Sarah's face got distant, and she shrugged. "Lekorh is lecturing Kromir about sleeping with you."

"Is it an authorization issue?"

Sarah shook her head. "It is an uncle issue. He saw you born, and you are the closest to Alia that we have been so far."

"Ah. I guessed as much. Well, if all goes well, Alia will be here today."

Sarah grinned. "I know. I am so excited."

"Well, if they don't want to eat, I worked up an appetite." Remi winked.

Sarah chuckled, and her eyes gleamed. "I know how to get him down here, but he is going to be pissed."

Remi blinked, and she heard a distant groan followed by cursing.

"Damn it, Sarah!"

Remi whispered as she picked up her eating prongs. "What did you do?"

"A Saya trick. I told his mind he had just had an orgasm. It usually distracts him pretty well."

Remi's eyes widened as Lekorh stalked into the living area. He grabbed Sarah by the shoulders and kissed her before staring into her eyes for a few moments.

Sarah shook, and Remi knew the dazed look in her eyes. Apparently, Lekorh was taking revenge.

Kromir stepped into the space, his hair wet and his uniform in place.

Remi nodded, and then, she returned to the meal. Kromir joined her and sat across from her, his feet bracketing hers under the table.

Lekorh and Sarah sat down, and Sarah's cheeks had a definite pink tinge.

Remi smiled and took another serving of the first cheese omelette, settling it on her palm plate so that the endless cheese string didn't get weird.

Sarah explained the contents to the guys while Remi kept eating. She sipped at her tea and then returned to her meal.

Having used a dozen eggs, Remi was amused to see the food disappear so quickly. "Should I make more?"

Kromir nodded, and Remi got to her feet. Her head spun for a moment, but she shook it off.

She got two more omelettes onto the table in five minutes, and then, she had to stop and rest against the counter.

Sarah looked at her, and her eyes widened. "Remi?"

Remi was going to say something flippant, but instead, she collapsed on the floor.

She could feel herself being carried and then the hum and chirp of medical scanners.

The excited voices of the medical team told her what she

had not been thinking about. She was an accelerator with an embryo.

Kromir's voice was no-nonsense. "Extract them so that they cease to cause her distress."

Remi opened her eyes and looked around. There was a cluster of men at the display units for the scanners. Kromir wasn't one of them. She glanced down, and he was holding her hand.

"So, it was pregnancy that knocked me out?"

"Sarah said it was common in your species."

The medic turned to look at her, and there was awe in his expression. "I have never seen so many female embryos at one time."

Remi was nervous. "How many?"

Kromir murmured, "Five. All Mrek-Rrassic."

Remi nearly passed out again. She rallied. "How can they tell?"

"Genetic markers are distinctive even without the wings that emerge during puberty."

She exhaled and slid her hand over her abdomen. There was a slight bulge. "How fast are they growing?"

Kromir scowled. "Too fast for your system. Medics!"

She was mortified that he was at her side during the embryo retrieval, but holding his hand gave her something to do while she tried to ignore the crowd between her thighs.

The healing treatment commenced, and the medic stated, "I think, for the sake of her health, that she might want to take an inhibitor."

Kromir looked at Remi. "Would you like a break from the hormonal demands?"

She sighed. "I am going to think about it. I could just not have sex."

Kromir looked hurt. "I suppose that is an option."

The expression on his face was priceless. She chuckled,

and he smiled slightly, lifting her hand to his lips.

"Shouldn't you be *examining* something? This can't be on your schedule."

"No. Until the next portal opening, I am all yours."

She smiled. "Lucky me."

She paused. "We are going to need names. They will be going out on the next outbound transport."

Kromir nodded. "You are correct. What would you suggest?"

Remi chuckled. "How about, Emi, Mira, Mori, Kirro, and Rommi."

He smiled slowly. "You used our names."

"I did. Emi Remi-Kromir has a nice ring to it."

He nodded and kissed her hand again. "It does."

She chuckled and let the med centre do its work to undo the torn tissues and ripped muscle that the little darlings had created. It seemed the only way that her family was going to keep growing would involve the canisters that held their embryos. It was not something that she had hoped for, but at least, she was aligned with the right species to help her out.

Outside the port, she thought about the visit to the gestation centre two hours earlier. Their babies were already visible blobs and growing fast. They were probably going to have to start some kind of gene therapy to stop the Bree-Arix line from spreading wide enough to take over other worlds, but for now, the Rrassic doctors and researchers were delighted.

Kromir was wearing his official posture, and she was standing as near to the portal as she could get. Lekorh and Sarah were there to wait for their daughter, as well as monitor the parade that was about to emerge. Medics were standing by for the stabilization shots.

Remi watched as the port controller opened their end of

the tunnel between dimensions, and then, she waited.

The first one of her siblings to walk through the portal was Brer. He grinned and kept walking toward the waiting medics. The children that she had watched grow up were now adults through their Nool phase, and they came through at a steady pace until there was a pause.

Remi tensed. There shouldn't be a pause.

Lekorh straightened. "Remi, Alia says you need to sing."

Remi moved as close to the portal as she could be, and she sang. Every pop song from her mother's homeworld that she could remember came out of her mouth and the extra vocal cords that she rarely used vibrated as she commanded the Rrassic to come to her.

She sang and ignored what was going on around her. The first Rrassic to step through had a dazed expression, and she turned him toward the medics. The same with the woman after him. She would hug them all when this was over, but there were three faces she was longing to see.

When Bree stumbled through, she smiled at Remi and then headed for the medics. Alia was next, and Sarah gasped. Remi's father came through last, and Remi's voice broke. She hugged him as he cleared the portal, and he squeezed her tight.

"You have pulled quite the audience, Remi."

She focused on the spot where the portal used to be. "I am not looking."

Arix turned her, and she saw that every Rrassic in the port had come to her call. The overseer was scowling at her; Isabella looked confused. Remi's gaze went to Kromir, and he was staring at her in shock.

She swallowed, and her throat throbbed. "Dad. Go and get your shot."

He nodded and walked over to where the other members of the first generation were hugging each other and clapping shoulders in relief.

Alia was standing in front of her parents, and her third eye was open. It was the same lovely gold as her father's.

They moved as one, and their hug was so sweet, it moved Remi to tears.

"So, you also have a siren's call." Kromir was standing in front of her.

"A what?"

"You can summon folk at will."

She shook her head. "No. Only Rrassic and hybrids."

He stared at her in shock. "You know about this?"

"Of course. They are my extra vocal cords, but you can't see them on a scan unless I turn my head."

He gripped her shoulders. "You should have told me."

"Why? I thought you would learn about it eventually."

"Because it makes you more than a hybrid. You now have a weapon. A weapon that can be used against the Rrassic."

"Or for it. I don't know who you are, but why are you holding my daughter?" Bree was scowling, and Arix matched her expression.

Remi hadn't heard them approach.

"Examiner Kromir, these are my parents. Bree and Arix. Mom, Dad, this is Kromir. He is the one who did the assessments on the hybrids and pronounced them successful."

Arix let out a deep breath. "It still does not explain why he is touching you."

Kromir released her and bowed. "I greet you as the current mate to your daughter and father of her children."

Bree brightened. "Children?"

Kromir nodded. "Five. They were extracted this morning and have dramatically increased their developmental pace."

Bree swayed. "Five? I thought three at a time was rough."

Arix frowned. "Why did you let her conceive so many?"

Kromir was being faced with an angry father who was

rippling with colour.

"I did not know she was capable of being receptive to stimulation."

Remi blushed. Her father and Kromir argued, saying that he was responsible for her multiple issue without verifying that she was pregnant or not. In Arix's eyes, Kromir should have had a portable scanner on standby so that they would have stopped at one.

Bree and Arix had it down to a fine art after their first eight children. The second set of triplets was enough of a scare to make Arix take it very seriously.

He was now passing that knowledge to Kromir.

"And what is this about *current mate*? You either are, or you aren't."

"Dad, he works for the council. He doesn't live on Imrahl, and I don't know where I will end up either."

Her father scowled. He was good at scowling. "Mates should remain together."

Bree put her hand on his arm. "Yes, they should. Now, let's go get everyone settled. Lianne and Sorrok want to meet their first batch before they have to head out with the next ones."

Niiva and Argo arrived to greet their children. Their daughter distracted Iktabi and Isabella. And Lianne and Sorrok had to listen to their entire brood trying to talk at once.

Remi hugged her parents, and then, she did what she used to do when she used her voice in front of strangers. She bolted.

CHAPTER TEN

Remi needed some time to think about the shock on Kromir's face. When she passed the gathered Rrassic outside the port, she told them, "As you were."

They followed her command and returned to their daily assignments. She used their movement to get lost in the crowd, shifting her colouration to make her appear to be a human woman. She was a tall human woman but still human, nonetheless.

The scent of pastries pulled her into the market. She just needed a moment to think, and sweets were right up her alley.

She walked into the teashop and looked at the selection, biting her lip when she was spoiled for choice.

A human woman smiled at her. "Can I help you?"

Remi nodded. "It is my first time here, so what would you recommend?"

"I will pick a few things. Bad day?"

She blinked. "Good and bad, but it just started."

"Right. Have a seat and leave it to me." The woman grinned.

Remi glanced over her shoulder and located a seat with a chair against the wall and a delicate table. She settled herself, and the server brought out three pastries and a cup of tea.

"On the house. Nobody deserves a bad day."

Remi inclined her head. "Thank you. Thank the proprietor, too."

The woman grinned. "You can see him peeping around

the corner?"

"Yes."

"Well, I hear a lot of gossip, and I don't remember seeing you before. I would have noticed. I am guessing that you are one of the hybrids that the Rrassic have been whispering about."

Remi arranged the pastries in the order she wanted to eat them. "Interesting guess."

"Well, it is nice to know that the humans mating with the Rrassic might eventually come up with something like you. What was your mother's species?"

The woman went from conspiratorial to curious.

Remi let her camouflage fade, and she looked at the woman. "Nothing that you have ever heard of."

The server gasped and nodded, smiling as she returned to serving the other customers.

The Rrassic knew what she was the moment that her colouration was restored. They warily inclined their heads toward her. She ignored them and bit into the first pastry.

It just showed her that she had been too wrapped up in enjoying her time with Kromir. For a few hours, she had forgotten what she was.

She was midway into the second pastry when a familiar face arrived, and Remi sighed and sat back. She inclined her head to her friend and smiled. "Alia. It is good to see you home."

Alia came up to her and gave her a hug with her third eye wide open. She was a woman now, but she looked so young to Remi's eyes.

"That is just because you are an old, bitchy cow." Alia smiled as they parted.

Remi laughed, and her friend pulled up a chair. The server arrived and stared at Alia. "What can I get for you?"

"A Vedder special and Sarah's pastry, please, Dot." Alia

smiled brightly at the woman.

"Have you been in before?"

Alia shook her head. "No, but a friend has familiarized me with your menu. My compliments to Sommin."

Dot was flustered, but she went to get the pastries.

Remi blinked. "Don't tell me. This is *that* pastry shop."

"Yeah. The one where my mom meeting my dad became inevitable."

Remi nodded and returned to her snack. "I am very glad you made it. What happened?"

"Tobin balked. It was only for a second, but it warped the pathway. I knew they would find you, so I sent my dad the message."

"Right. I am glad everyone made it."

"It was weird to leave everything in the warehouse, but the next group needs a clean slate, so to speak."

Remi remembered packing. It had only been three Imrahl days ago, but it felt a lifetime ago.

"So, did we get the positive assessment?" Alia smiled as Dot brought her order in.

"I am sure your father told you, but yes, we did."

"Before you slept with him?"

Remi coughed. "Yes."

"He didn't know about your voice, did he?"

"No."

"Why not?"

Remi felt her face heat. "You know I don't like using it."

"It is a tremendous tactical advantage. You can get orders to our kind within a kilometre of your location. They come when you call and go where you tell them."

"It is a blunt-force object that makes them do what I say."

"It is a tool to move forces. To keep them safe."

Remi teared up. "I have really missed you."

"Don't say that too loudly. My parents are following with

your parents and your new mate. Are you going to keep him?" There was speculation in Alia's voice.

"If you go near him, I will swat you."

Alia chuckled. "So, you are keeping him."

"If I can. None of us knows the rules on that yet."

She was onto her third pastry when Sarah and Lekorh walked in, leading the others.

The teashop emptied of its regulars in under a minute.

Alia smiled. "Keep your head up, cousin. It will be fine."

Remi watched as her elders took up a perimeter watch and Kromir came toward her. Alia passed him, and she checked him out from head to toe as she went. Her expression was one of approval. If Remi didn't want him, she might take him for a spin.

Remi was smiling as she looked at Kromir, and when she saw his expression, the smile faded.

He sat next to her. "You should not have run."

"I know. I needed time to think."

"You did not mention you were a siren. Did you ever use your voice on me?"

She gasped, and before she knew it, she hit him across the face with her fist. His head snapped to the side, and she smelled blood.

"I am taking that as a negative."

"I would never use the voice for that. Did you come out of any moment feeling dazed or as if you didn't belong there?"

He blinked and smiled, showing the blood on his teeth. "Once or twice."

"Then, it wasn't me, jackass. I summon and they come. They know they are called, and they come anyway."

Kromir nodded. "I see. What is your distance?"

"Depending on the environment, a kilometre. I had to call in many of my brothers, sisters, and cousins over the years."

"Do any of your siblings share the talent?"

"I believe two of my sisters have it. You would have to ask my parents."

Kromir glanced over at Arix and Bree. "I will do it later."

She chuckled. "It would have developed after I left, so I can only go by what I saw when they were adolescents."

"I see. This is excellent news. I am now the only examiner in five decades and a dozen worlds to meet a siren."

She smiled slightly. "I prefer alternatively vocal."

Her mother and Sarah snorted. She had confirmed that they were close enough to listen.

He frowned.

She grinned. "Human joke about deliberate classification."

"Ah. We are going to have to speak to the council."

Remi nodded. "I know."

"No. Today. I am filing the request for a portal as soon as I am able."

Lekorh raised his voice. "Request is filed. Waiting for the window."

Bree looked around. "What is happening?"

Arix squeezed his mate's hand. "Remi is going to work."

Bree exhaled slowly. "Right. Of course."

Remi smiled encouragingly at her mother. This was the hard part. Letting go.

She finished her pastry and smiled before sipping her tea. "Okay, so, my last day on Imrahl. I am glad I ate dessert first."

Sarah got up and walked into the back, having a discussion with the baker.

She came back and winked at those who remained. "We are getting some takeout. Where is a good place to hash this out?"

Lekorh looked up. "Departure in two hours."

Sarah lifted her head. "Change of plans, Sommin. Can we

use your teashop?"

The burly Nool appeared from behind the doorway. "Dot, come with me. We are going shopping for ingredients for tomorrow. For . . ."

Sarah smiled. "Two hours."

"Two hours." He smiled and ushered his curious assistant out of the shop.

Sarah locked the doors, and she spread her arms. "We now have privacy for two hours. So, Bree and Arix, your girl is going to meet the council and hopefully be tapped as representative for Imrahl."

Kromir shook his head. "That is now unlikely. Sirens belong in battle. They won't take the chance of putting one as powerful as she is on a council."

Lekorh frowned. "I am bringing Iktabi in on this."

Three minutes later, Iktabi, Isabella, and their daughter, Sable, entered the teashop, and Sarah locked up again.

Sable shrieked happily and ran to Remi for a hug. "I missed you."

"I know. Watch the wings, sweetie. You don't want to knock anyone over."

Sable chuckled and folded her wings tightly against her back. "Sorry. I am so glad you called us through."

"I am glad I was there to do it."

"Father says you are going to be leaving."

Iktabi nodded from behind his daughter.

Sable smiled. "He thinks he has an idea to keep you from active duty unless you want to go. It will keep you separate from the rest of the Rrassic."

Remi looked to him with a quirked brow. "You have an idea, Overseer?"

"I do. General Remi Bree-Arix of Imrahl."

Kromir's breath whooshed out of him before he started laughing. "That would do it."

The Rrassic males were grinning, and even Alia had delight in her eyes.

Remi waited until the laughing subsided, and she cocked her head. "Does anyone want to explain this to me?"

Iktabi nodded. "Yes, but I will explain it while you are outfitted with rank insignia and a proper uniform. Kromil is going to have to work like a fiend on this one."

Kromir looked delighted. "He is here? I wondered where he ended up."

Isabella smiled. "Best clothing construction on Imrahl."

Remi blinked. "The clock is ticking as mom says. Where do we need to go?"

Their entire party evacuated the teashop, taking the pastries along, and moved the invasion to the tailor's shop. Kromir's words made sense when she saw Kromil. They had come from the same genetic source. It was obvious. For lack of a better term, they were brothers.

Kromil was informed as to their requirements, and she was stripped, measured, and the fabricators started whirring before her boots had time to cool.

One hour after they had arrived in the shop, Sable had designed a rank insignia for Imrahl, and a cluster of them was on each shoulder of the graceful tunic that mimicked her earlier clothing.

In twelve hours, she had gone from hybrid to mother to general. She was a bit nervous about what the rest of the day was going to bring.

Alia stepped out from behind the curtain wearing the mark of the Saya on her shoulders. "I am coming with you. You will need a communicator, and I am connected to my parents and all the siblings that will come. Though you also have Kromir, you are not going out there alone."

Lekorh was holding Sarah, but though they appeared sad, they were also bursting with pride.

"I will be happy to have you, Ally."

Kromir nodded. "We have half an hour to get to the portal at the new city."

Remi looked from Alia to Kromir. "Can you carry us both?"

He nodded. "I will need to drop from a rooftop."

Alia grinned and glanced at her parents. "I know just the one."

They grabbed the packs of clothing that Kromil had created, watched as the two brothers shared a handclasp, and then, they were running through the Imrahl afternoon toward the admin building.

They had a portal to catch.

CHAPTER ELEVEN

R emi was expecting to be greeted by weapons, but the entire council had shown up for their arrival. Not a weapon in sight.

Kromir stepped forward, and he inclined his head respectfully. "Gentlemen of the Rrassic council, I present General Remi Bree-Arix of Imrahl, siren of the Rrassic and first hybrid."

The council murmured, and the representatives of the different branches of the species looked impressed.

Kromir continued. "At her side is Advisor Alia Sarah-Lekorh, Saya-Rrassic-human hybrid, and temporal communicator."

Alia stood next to Remi with her head high and shoulders back.

There were two Rrassic that Remi hadn't seen before. An aquatic Rrassic with silvery green skin and gills prominently displayed on his mostly bare torso. The crimson Rrassic with black hair was not one covered by the basic common listings.

So, this made the seven branches of the Rrassic. As they primarily reproduced via cloning, the branches were probably very direct lines.

The Zjin-Rrassic councillor looked them over. "Both female?"

She twisted her lips. "How astute of you to observe that."

The councillors' expressions varied from amused to irritated.

The Regiz smiled. "I do not mind that they are female. It

seems an excellent situation."

Remi held up her hand. "This situation has just begun five Mrek daughters. I have chosen my mate, and whether we reproduce again will not change my focus."

The eyes of the council focused on Kromir.

He nodded, "All reports have been turned in to Ndoro."

The Mrek councillor nodded. "He has. I just was unaware of the full nature of his mate. You say she is a siren?"

Kromir said, "She is. I have seen the evidence for myself, and others of her bloodline carry the same characteristic."

Alia asked, "Are we to conduct the interview here? Or shall we proceed to the council chambers? Imrahl has already been notified of our arrival."

The Saya looked at Alia, and she looked at him calmly with all three eyes open.

Remi watched the stare-down and could only imagine what was going on on the psychic plain.

Alia stood with her feet firmly planted on the landscape of her mind. "You have entered without requesting entrance."

The head of the Saya looked at her with curiosity. "You nearly kept me out. That is not something most of my trainees can manage."

"Congratulations on walking on your own. I hear that many of our kind shun their own bodies."

The Saya councillor looked at her with narrowed eyes. "You seem to know a lot."

"My father has been an excellent instructor, as has my mother. I know why the council met us, and I have to tell you that we are no threat to the Rrassic. We are here for your survival."

"You threaten our survival." He scowled and approached her.

"We are your survival. Remi's daughters are proof of it. They are fully Mrek on the genetic level. They are the next generation of Rrassic with functioning reproductive systems and a slightly shorter lifespan. When the threat of the Voboth is over, they will be ready to strike out among the stars."

"You seem very sure of yourself, hybrid."

"I have trained every minute of every day to learn how the Rrassic think, act, and what they want for their future. You want what any species want—triumph, a future, and survival." She smiled. "Having one without the others is meaningless."

"Would you and the siren agree to being neutralized while we look into the matter?"

Alia cocked her head. "Her daughters have already been decanted. Contact Lekorh for details on their status."

"I cannot move my mind through time, as you know."

She sighed. "Elder Councillor Ramor, I know. The reports on you were very detailed. Are you really wearing an armored framework under your suit?"

He looked down at his silvery skin, naked body, and dark tattoos that covered his chest and shoulders, even in his psychic projection, he was wearing his Saya rank marks.

She looked down at her own skin, and it was just the soft pinkish silver that she was used to. No marks for her. She wasn't a traditionally trained Saya.

"How did you gain your control?"

"My cousins allowed me to practice on them. It was supervised, and any unusual activity was stopped immediately, but it let me understand how people think and why they hide information."

"What do you mean, 'cousins'?"

"It was decided early on that all hybrids address each other as cousin. It emphasizes our connection and minimizes the impact of our being raised by other couples if our parents are not available for the creche."

"You had contact with your parents." He seemed surprised.

"I did. My father linked with me directly when I was a few cells. When I gained consciousness, he knew, and he helped me through everything when he could. Except my homework. That was always ten days too late." She smiled in fond remembrance.

"You have affection for your genetic donors."

"We do. And our caregivers. We know that we were created in unions of mutual affection and desire. We were wanted for more than our destiny as weapons and warriors. Two people cared for each other and made us. Other couples raised us with the knowledge that we are wanted and needed. The younger children and older children around us let us know what we might become if we practice and remind us to teach the next generation. There is always another generation coming after us, as Remi has proved."

Elder Ramor shook his head in amazement. "Stable with complete awareness. It is amazing that your mother was able to keep her sanity."

"She was an empath before an accident rewired her for telepathy, so she was always aware of the minds of others. It has been hard for her to send her children off to be raised by others, but she does it gladly, knowing what the end game will be."

He paused. "None of us know what it will be."

She inclined her head to him. "You have not met my mother. She has run the permutations and combinations for the likelihood of success and is confident that the majority of the hybrids will survive."

"What of the Rrassic?"

"Evolution is change, and adding new genetic patterns

will bring that change to the Rrassic. Keep your seven divisions, we will blur the lines and be the greater for it." Alia smiled and showed her teeth.

She lowered her canines for the display, and his eyes opened wide. She spoke carefully. "Within each hybrid is every possibility of the Rrassic, and while some characteristics are visible, others can rise when needed. Remi has the intelligence of a Dorbin, the strength of a Zjin, the stealth of a Luthin, and the voice of a siren. She wears it all with good humour and the sex drive of a Regiz. She has been made a general because she can command troops, and they will listen. She puts herself between the innocent and danger as a reflex, and she always has. She was a big sister to me when I was growing up, and when she left, the last ten years at the creche dragged. She is the key to mobilizing the hybrids and making them into a fighting force to be reckoned with. If you ignore her and her potential, you will regret it."

She waved her hand, and they were sitting in the teashop where her mother had worked.

"Shall we continue this with some refreshments?"

The elder nodded, and she served tea while they discussed the future of the hybrids and their possibilities in regards to the survival of the Rrassic. In the real world, a few seconds went by, and when they came to an agreement, they finished their snacks, stood, and returned to their companions.

Remi smiled when Alia's third eye faded to normal. She was home again.

Alia nodded toward the Saya and the Dorbin who were standing close while the Dorbin listened to what the Saya was silently saying.

The Dorbin nodded. "I understand. We will have to speak

to the rest of the council. Examiner Kromir, please, take them to the boardroom for refreshments while we discuss this information."

Remi looked at Kromir, and he smiled reassuringly. That look went a long way to keeping her calm.

"Remi, Alia, this way."

Kromir walked past the council, and they parted for their party. Remi followed her mate's wings, and Alia was at her back.

They entered the boardroom, and the dispenser was waiting. Kromir went to the unit, and he kept his back to her. "If you were curious about how the council works, I would suggest that you go and find out, but make sure that no one knows you are there."

Remi blinked and went invisible. She left Alia with Kromir and sprinted silently down the hall to enter the council chamber as the door swung closed.

She listened to the Zjin saying, "They are dangerous. It was a mistake to choose the humans."

The Regiz lounged in his seat at the round table, and he shrugged. "I liked them. They are strong. Very strong."

The Zjin growled. "That is not the point. They could destroy us."

The Dorbin cocked his head. "Why would they?"

The Saya was sitting still and watching the proceedings.

The crimson male looked her way, but his gaze didn't stop. She pulled in her senses and simply crouched against the wall.

They debated back and forth, bringing up reports and data sheets on the humans and other species that were producing hybrids. The humans were able to withstand drastic temporal interference, so they had a leg up in development. The other species would be ready within the year, but the humans would have a fighting population in the next forty-five days if the breeding continued on its upward trend.

The Zjin finally said, "What will ensure that the hybrids take orders?"

The Saya smiled. "Open your minds, and I will tell you what I learned from the little Saya."

She didn't have time to put up a heavier shield; she was swept into the psychic realm with them.

The Saya saw her, and he laughed. "So, you were in the room."

The crimson Rrassic laughed. "She was barely there, but it was noticeable if you were looking for the heat signature in the floor."

Remi stood, naked as she always was when she was a projection. "Fine. Yes. I was in the room. I know how the Im-rahl Rrassic function, but you guys like to talk."

The Saya snorted. "Allow me to show you my conversation with her companion."

The words and emotions of Alia spilled over all of them. Remi smiled as the images of her and the little three-eyed child were broadcast to the gathered men.

They understood the bonds of brotherhood, but sister-hood was a different situation.

"This is why we are safe with the hybrids. They are not all male. They are from a cooperative society. They are not violent by nature; they are protective of each other, as they were raised to be." The Saya was grinning.

Remi looked at Alia's memories floating in the air. She smiled at the ones she was in and sighed at the ones she had missed.

She stood naked in an ancient temple styled in graceful lines with seven nude men. They were looking at her and feeling Alia's memories run through them.

"This is why we are going to fight, and why we will win. We are not fighting for glory or money or fame. We are fighting so that there is a chance that our youngest cousins won't have to. If they can be born into Imrahl, directly from the canisters and raised by their own parents without the pressure for multiple children, we will be pleased with how our lives have turned out. We just want our start. What happens next can be dealt with after the survival of the Rrassic, and its chosen races are assured. We will defend you if you let us."

The seven faces looked at her and then at each other.

Finally, the Dorbin nodded. "We accept your offer and that of the human hybrids. We will exit the psychic realm and enter into a contract where both parties will be represented. Saya, end this excursion."

Remi stood straight and resumed her visibility. The Dorbin-Rrassic got up and walked over to her, extending his hand. "Welcome to the Rrassic council, Remi Bree-Arix, siren of Imrahl, General of the hybrids."

She clasped his arm and exhaled slowly. This is what she had trained for. Time to negotiate.

Chapter Twelve

Remi sat with Elder Theth, the Dorbin, Elder Ramor of the Saya, and Elder Vresk of the Pilar, the man who was built for fire. Kromir and Alia were sitting on her side of the table.

"So, we are negotiating what the hybrids will be responsible for. Well, the human hybrids. The rest of them will be taken care of as their abilities and needs are assessed."

The recorder was broadcasting all of the events to the Overseers on different worlds.

Remi took a deep breath. "First things first. The human hybrids of Imrahl pledge themselves to the support and defense of the Rrassic species. In return, we get the rights and responsibilities of full citizens."

Elder Theth blinked. "Interesting."

"When a sufficient number of Imrahl or other hybrids have been generated, a warship will be provided by the Rrassic to be controlled by the general leading the hybrids at the time."

"Easily done. We have many ships lying empty with insufficient warriors to man them."

That was a surprise. "Well, on to a wage."

They haggled back and forth but eventually settled on what Arix had drummed into Remi as a standard pay scale for the Rrassic.

Remi cleared her throat. "We have settled dwellings, food, and occupation as well as advancement opportunities. Now, let's talk about sex."

The elders looked shocked. Kromir was amused, but he knew this question was coming.

"Breeding is a concern. Our parents were required to be a match between human and Rrassic. What about the hybrids? Are they required to seek a breeding partner or lover only among their own? Should they seek out the Rrassic? Or is any relationship fine as long as it is registered? How many children are acceptable? We don't want to breed out the Rrassic. Our parents were asked to produce twenty individual genetic pairings. How many will the hybrids be allowed to create?"

The three council members deliberated, and finally, they came to a consensus.

Theth spelled it out. "The hybrids of Imrahl will be required to log their genetic pattern in case of injury or death. That is non-negotiable. If they choose a breeding partner, they must also be recorded."

Remi wondered where he was going with that.

"An imprint of your memories will also be taken by a recording Saya in case of accidental injury or death. This goes for any of your crew who have paired up in any way."

This was getting odd.

"In the event of your body ceasing to function, a new clone will be generated using accelerated techniques, and your mind will be loaded into the body so that you may resume your duties."

"That isn't necessary . . ." she started to explain, but Kromir gripped her hand.

"It is necessary. This council is not elected, it is eternal. As you join our ranks, even as you insist on taking action, you are joining us as long as the Rrassic are alive. From this moment forward, there will always be a Remi Bree-Arix, her mate Kromir, and her advisor Alia on the council."

Remi looked to Kromir, and he nodded. Alia simply

shrugged.

She blinked. "Right. Okay, what about the mating for the rest of the hybrids?"

"They may mate with Rrassic or other hybrids provided that they run through a genetic assessment for suitability. It is fine for now, but the lines of relations may blur over time."

She nodded. "Acceptable. Now, the number of offspring?"

"A limit of five unless otherwise authorized. Each authorization will occur on a case-by-case basis."

Remi looked at Kromir, and he winked.

She took a deep breath. "While the creche is acceptable in an emergency situation, some families would like to raise their own offspring at a leisurely pace."

"That will also be analyzed on a case-by-case basis. The more demanding occupations cannot spare the time to raise offspring."

Remi blinked. "Right. It will be a case-by-case situation but determined by the parents, not the council. A week in the creche is enough to raise a child, even in a demanding occupation."

She drummed her fingers on the table. "Now, birth control. The women are slowed or the men are?"

She waited while the council chattered again.

"Both. We will slow the fertility of both the male and female members of the union. If they still conceive after that, their authorization will be reconsidered. If science can't stop them, who are we to restrict them?"

She smiled. "Excellent."

The council members looked at her, and Elder Vresk spoke quietly. "Now, tell us why you are willing to fight for the Rrassic."

Remi cocked her head and smiled. "My mother. Well, not

my mother, but all the original humans who were sampled. Those women are living their lives on their homeworld, some are falling in love, some are barely surviving. Right now, they have the potential to do anything, be anyone, and to live a life that is only a possibility right now. If the Voboth get them, that possibility is over."

She straightened her shoulders. "My mother knows what she is. She knows she is a clone that has been altered to be compatible with the Rrassic. The other women gain this knowledge when they have mates and learn about the canisters and how the next generation will be raised. They may not like it, but they learn it."

She swallowed. "The idea that the Earth is sitting there with no idea that trouble is coming and that they are not going to be able to defend themselves makes me ill. It made my mother ill, as well as other females who learned of their origins. Once they accepted that they were cloned, they had to accept the approaching conflict. They might not have wanted us to be born for this, but we were. This is the hand that we were dealt, and every day that I spent with my mother, I knew that she was mourning the day I would leave for this purpose. She still raised my siblings and me with an eye toward the future and the hope that we would see it."

Kromir squeezed her hand.

"So, just because a human doesn't like a situation doesn't mean that they let it overtake them. The women that were selected were all highly adaptable. They are living with the knowledge that somewhere out there, the original person with their memories is living the same life that they remember being abducted from. They want a chance for them, too, and we are their best chance at survival, or so our fathers have told us."

The councillors paused as if that was not what they had expected. Well, two of them paused, Vresk was grinning.

The rest of the minutia was taken care of, and she signed the contract with her blood. Kromir and Alia signed as witnesses, and the councillors did the same.

She looked to Theth. "What happens now?"

"Now, we wait until there is a sufficient amount of warriors to man that warship."

She grinned. She wasn't sure that the Rrassic were aware of it, but she never specified the gender of the warriors. They were going to have a unisex fighting force. Being a hybrid was an equal opportunity event.

Kromir flew her over the staging area and showed her around the outpost.

"So, we are on a space station?"

"We are. Locking a portal onto the station is a tricky situation, but with enough Saya monitoring the connection, it is manageable."

She chuckled and let the air rush past her face. "I was surprised that they gave in on the warship."

"The first attack on our breeding world knocked our population down to a small percentage of what it used to be. We have all the equipment to wage war and no warriors to man them."

"And so the idea to use likely worlds to supply new genetic material was born."

He nodded and wheeled slowly. "We used the list that the Voboth had created. They fear a specific type of being, and humans were on the list. The worlds with potential were marked out, and we attempted contact with two of them. They rejected our efforts, and we moved on to less sophisticated worlds with hardy populations."

"And enter the Earth and its myriad humans."

"There was so much to learn about, so much to examine. We went as thorough as we could with the investigation, and while that was going on, we opened a temporal bubble around Imrahl. It let us build the facilities we needed and prepare the tanks to grow the population we required. We gathered Nool from a training centre, and their time on Imrahl aged them into proper Rrassic."

She smiled. "I wondered how that happened. My father used to say that time on Imrahl aged him until he met my mother."

"Arix was one of the few trackers who had been full Rrassic off world. He was considered an excellent genetic line for future hybrids. No one guessed he would be one of the first to find a mate."

"He was surprised as well. What is your thought on the matter of finding a mate?"

He chuckled and headed back to their quarters under the huge dome of the city in space.

"My thought is that if I knew what I was in for, I would have gone to Imrahl a day earlier."

She giggled and felt the warmth of affection running through her soul. "I would have left the creche earlier, too. One whole day, or five years. Either way, a minute is too long to wait for you."

They landed on the roof, and he carried her into their quarters. She smiled when he set her on her feet, and she looked into his hot copper gaze.

"Do you think they are recording this?"

He shrugged and removed his tunic. "Yes, General, I believe that they are."

She grinned and removed her own clothing with rapid movements. "Fine. Let them watch. But I get to be on top."

He laughed, and when they were naked, she pushed him back, crawling carefully until she was straddling him.

She rubbed herself against him and used everything she had learned about him to tease both of them until joining their bodies was the only way to stop the fire in their blood.

Lying in his arms, she stroked a hand over his chest. "How much time do we have?"

"A week at the most. Alia has told me that they have over two thousand canisters heading to the creche. There has been a surge of receptive humans, and the multiple births are speeding things along."

"And I have been slowed to a crawl. I don't feel any different."

"Neither do I and everything else works just fine. I was worried about that."

She laughed. "I wasn't. It takes more than messing with fertility to stop us."

"It won't stop me from trying to override their controls." He chuckled and ran his fingers through her hair.

"I look forward to your efforts. Will you be on my first mission when the warship launches?"

"No. I work for the Rrassic council. You are the hybrid, General. I am not allowed to be in a battle situation." He didn't seem pleased about that.

"Don't worry. I will keep myself safe. I promise not to do anything stupid and to keep our daughters in mind when I do go into battle. Them and all of the others in the next generation."

He gave her a squeeze. "That is all I can ask. Well, General, is it my turn?"

She grinned. "By all means, this time you have to do all the work."

He eased her over and moved to cover her, his wings blocking the light in the room.

She was warm and cozy in the bit of privacy made for two, and she was going to savour the moment. She had the inkling that privacy would be hard to come by in the months and years ahead.

For now, she was with her mate, and the future was bright.

EPILOGUE

Remi stood on the command deck of the *Hunted Heart*. It was the Imrahl hybrid flagship, and she was proud to be commanding it.

Kromir came through on the com. "You are approaching the Voboth raiding party. Prepare to engage."

She nodded. "Weapon systems online. Defense systems online. Come around this moon and prepare to kick some ass."

The crew was intent on their stations, but they all had a feral grin as they moved the ship into position and got the readouts.

"Five hostiles firing."

"Return fire." She sat and watched as her ship drew the bulk of the Voboth's fire.

Alia's voice in her mind made her smile. *Birthday surprise coming up.*

The moon next to them began a stream of fire that caught the Voboth broadside. The Rrassic skill at slowing and speeding time at a fixed point worked very well when they had ambush points.

Alia and the hybrid Saya-Rrassic were doing amazing work in seeking out the areas where the Voboth were planning ambushes. They just made it their mission to get hybrid troops there first.

Remi watched her screens and sent orders to get the backup ships into the best positions for disabling the Voboth ships. They wanted to capture one of the hierarchy, and rumor had it that there was a Yoboth on one of the vessels.

"Scan the ships. Look for the target. Check for captured species."

When the ships were still moving forward but had no power, the *Hunted Heart* was moved to attach to the main vessel. Matching the speed was easy for her pilot, but Sreena had always been good at special navigation.

They docked lightly, and Remi got up, arming herself for a walk through the Voboth vessel.

She put on her breather and comlinks, smiling as she heard, "Kromir is ordering you to be safe."

She laughed. "He does remember that I outrank him, right?"

"He says he doesn't give a rat's ass." The com officer chuckled.

"Excellent. Excuse me. I have to earn my keep." She went down to the point of connection, and she slid down the ladder, into the captured vessel.

Remi pulled out her batons and walked with six of her crewmen through the dark halls of the ship. Life signs were up ahead, and she saw the wobble that indicated Voboth.

She didn't run toward the signals. She walked deliberately and confidently until the Voboth tried to jump her little group. At that point, she used the electroshock in her batons and then unleashed decades of combat training until she had broken the neck of the attacker.

Once her opponent was disabled, she assisted her crew and sent the injured member back to the ship.

They searched the ship, level by level. The Yoboth was found on one of the shuttles. The message came through the coms, and Remi acknowledged it. There were still life signs on the ship, and they weren't going to leave them to die in the darkness.

Remi noted the strong burn of the life signs, and she

whispered, "Not Voboth."

The crew behind her acknowledged, and they changed their postures from defensive to on guard.

Remi found the door and used a digital lock pick to open it.

As the door slid past, the biosignatures rushed toward it. Remi stood to one side and simply stuck out her foot.

Three men fell out, one on top of the other.

Remi crouched and examined the one that landed on top, and she blinked. Handsome, charcoal skin, and rich silver hair. His ears were as pointed as hers were, but she didn't recognize the species.

"Hello." She spoke calmly.

The men struggled to their feet and took up defensive postures. She straightened and looked at them curiously. They were tall, but they had the lean body type of adolescents. The first of them looked at her with crimson eyes. "Who are you? What are you doing here?"

She smiled. "We are the Rrassic. We are here to fight the Voboth. Who are you?"

They were speaking English, which was slightly confusing, but as all of the hybrids spoke it, it made communication easy.

The first male cleared his throat. "I am Prince Keigo. The Voboth have been holding me for ransom."

Remi contacted Alia and asked her to seek out verification.

"What is your species?"

"Limoor. We are from Limoor."

Alia's mental voice was clear. *Fourth planet on the Voboth attack plan.*

"You are reading my surface thoughts."

The prince blinked. "How did you notice?"

"The language you chose." She nodded. "Right. Back to the ship. We will get you home."

The prince was surprised. "You will?"

"We will. Our people face the same enemy. Getting you home might be a good step toward a diplomatic relationship. Come this way."

She walked, and from behind, one of them blurted, "You are a female!"

She grinned and kept walking. Two of the crew bracketing them were also female. It was going to be a bit of a shock.

She climbed up the ladder and was lifted up and to the side. "Kromir, what the hell are you doing here?"

He growled and removed her breathing mask. "I arrived half an hour ago only to be told that you were doing your own sweep of the ship below."

She was pinned up against him with one of his wings blocking their view from the rest of the crew. "It was necessary. We only had one casualty. Yimith twisted his ankle in combat."

He growled low and pressed his head to hers.

"Excuse me. Are you the commander of this vessel?" Prince Keigo was next to them. He was addressing Kromir.

He shook his head. "I am an examiner for the Rrassic council."

He reluctantly released Remi. She chuckled.

"My mate is General Remi Bree-Arix, hybrid siren of the Rrassic."

The prince was confused. "She cannot be in charge."

Remi was amused. "Why not?"

"You are female. Females are to be protected."

She sighed and stepped around to face him. She grabbed him by twisting her fists in his tunic and lifted him above her head. She held him there for thirty seconds until he started squirming. "If you want to see what the hybrid Rrassic can do, you are welcome to join combat practice in the atrium."

The crew took the three aliens away to guest quarters.

Kromir was sheepish. "I am sorry. I was worried."

"Well, you will have to get over it. We are at war, and I was bred for this position. My life and my actions are not my own. I must and will carry things through. Now, we have to get those Limoor home."

Kromir paused. "Limoor?"

"Yes. Prince Keigo is of the Limoor."

He kissed her quickly. "Excellent. The Rrassic have been trying to open discussions with them for a decade. You might have just stumbled upon the key."

She grabbed him by the back of the neck and held him to her to return the kiss before whispering, "Stumbled my ass. This mission has yielded a Yoboth and an in with a new species. Humanity was always good at war; us hybrids are going to take it to a new level."

She felt the internal giggle that was Alia's, and she batted her cousin away. This moment was all hers. They had inherited war, and she was going to enjoy that inheritance.

Author's Note

So, it looks like the war has started while the series ends. But, do I want to write a new series about the hybrids and their adventures? Really?

Do the readers want it? A new series is annoying for most folks, and I have been trying to finish things up.

I will let folks decide. Find the Viola's Readers group on Facebook and let me know.

This could be a long-running series. There will be a lot of hybrids and even more Rrassic and new species to find love in the stars with. I suppose that I will depend on the readers to decide. My editor is all for a new series and is laughing at me for backing myself into a corner. Look for it in late 2019.

Thanks for reading,

Viola Grace

ABOUT THE AUTHOR

Viola Grace (aka Zenina Masters) is a Canadian sci-fi/ paranormal romance writer with ambitions to keep writing for the rest of her life. She specializes in short stories because the thrill of discovery, of all those firsts, is what keeps her writing.

An artist who enjoys a story that catches you up, whirls you around, and sets you down with a smile on your face is all she endeavours to be. She prefers to leave the drama to those who are better suited to it, she always goes for the cheap laugh.

In real life, she now is engaged in beekeeping, and her adventures can be found on the YouTube channel, Mystery Bees Apiary. Just look for the cartoon kittens.